I'm Travis McGee. An artifact, genus boat bum, a pale-eyed, shambling, gangling, knuckly man, without enough unscarred hide left to make a decent lampshade. Watchful appraiser of the sandy-rumpled beach ladies. Creaking knight errant, yawning at the thought of the next dragon. They don't make grails the way they used to.

**BUT THIS TIME
I WAS GOING FOR A
DRAGON OF MY OWN.**

Fawcett Gold Medal Books
in the Travis McGee Series
by John D. MacDonald

THE DEEP BLUE GOOD-BYE 14176 $1.95
NIGHTMARE IN PINK 14259 $1.95
A PURPLE PLACE FOR DYING 14219 $1.95
THE QUICK RED FOX 14264 $1.75
A DEADLY SHADE OF GOLD 14221 $1.95
BRIGHT ORANGE FOR THE SHROUD 14243 $1.95
DARKER THAN AMBER 14162 $1.95
ONE FEARFUL YELLOW EYE 14146 $1.95
PALE GRAY FOR GUILT 14148 $1.95
DRESS HER IN INDIGO 14170 $1.75
THE LONG LAVENDER LOOK 13834 $1.95
A TAN AND SANDY SILENCE 14220 $1.95
THE SCARLET RUSE 13952 $1.95
THE TURQUOISE LAMENT 14200 $1.95
THE DREADFUL LEMON SKY 14148 $1.95
THE EMPTY COPPER SEA 14149 $2.25
THE GREEN RIPPER 14345 $2.50

8999

This offer expires 1/23/81

John D. MacDonald

THE GREEN RIPPER

FAWCETT GOLD MEDAL • NEW YORK

THE GREEN RIPPER

ISBN: 0-449-14345-7

Printed in the United States of America

First Fawcett Gold Medal printing: June 1980

10 9 8 7 6 5 4 3 2 1

To Maxwell P. Wilkinson
Representative and Friend

Fanaticism is described as redoubling your effort when you have forgotten your aim.

George Santayana

THE GREEN
RIPPER

1

Meyer came aboard *The Busted Flush* on a dark, wet, windy Friday afternoon in early December. I had not seen him in nearly two months. He looked worn and tired, and he had faded to an indoor pallor. He shucked his rain jacket and sat heavily in the biggest chair and said he wouldn't mind at all if I offered him maybe a little bourbon, one rock, a dollop of water.

"Where's Gretel?" he asked as I handed him his drink.

"Moved out," I said. He looked so dismayed I quickly added that she had found herself a job, finally, way the hell and gone over in the suburb of Tamarac, west of North Lauderdale and west of the

Turnpike, out in the area of the shiny new developments and shopping plazas, near University Community Hospital and Timber Run Golf Club. "Couldn't get any farther away and still be in the same metropolitan area. It takes at least forty minutes to drive over there."

"Doing what?"

"The outfit is called, excuse the expression, Bonnie Brae. It is a combination fat farm, tennis club, and real estate development. She works in the office, lives in one of the model houses, gives tennis lessons to the littlies, exercise classes for the fatties, and is becoming indispensable. She can tell you all about it. She'll be here about six or six thirty."

"I was afraid you two had split."

"No chance. I'm not going to let that one get away."

"Splendid judgment."

"It's a phase, Meyer. She did hard time in a bad marriage and says it stunted her. She has to make it on her own, she says, to become a complete person, and when she is, then we can think about what kind of arrangement we're going to have."

"Makes a certain amount of sense."

"Not to me."

"But you're not . . . being derisive or patronizing?"

"Hell, no. I am being full of understanding, and all that."

I didn't want to try to tell him what a vacuum

she left when she packed and moved out. The houseboat was dismally empty. When I woke up, if I wanted to hear clinking sounds from the galley, I had to go make them myself. The winter boats were beginning to come down, filling up the empty berths, spewing out their slender and elegant ladies to walk the area, shopping and smiling, providing what in times past had been like one of those commercial hatcheries where you pay a fee and catch your own trout and take it home to cook. But Grets had made all the pretty ladies look brittle, bloodless, and tasteless, and made the time without her seem leaden and endless.

In another season there were the girls of summer, robust and playful in their sandy ways, and now here were the winter ones, with cool surmise in the tended eye, fragrant and speculative, strolling and shopping, sailing and tanning, then making their night music and night scent, searching for something they could not quite name, but would know once they found it.

"How did the conference go?" I asked.

He shook a weary head. "These are bad days for an economist, my friend. We have gone past the frontiers of theory. There is nothing left but one huge ugly fact."

"Which is?"

"There is a debt of perhaps two trillion dollars out there, owed by governments to governments, by governments to banks, and there is not one chance in hell it can ever be paid back. There is not enough productive capacity in the world, plus enough raw materials, to provide maintenance of plant plus enough overage even to keep up with the mounting interest."

"What happens? It gets written off?"

He looked at me with a pitying expression. "All the major world currencies will collapse. Trade will cease. Without trade, without the mechanical-scientific apparatus running, the planet won't support its four billion people, or perhaps even half that. Agribusiness feeds the world. Hydrocarbon utilization heats and houses and clothes the people. There will be fear, hate, anger, death. The new barbarism. There will be plague and poison. And then the new Dark Ages."

"Should I pack?"

"Go ahead. Scoff. What the sane people and sane governments are trying to do is scuffle a little more breathing space, a little more time, before the collapse."

"How much time have we got?"

"If nobody pushes the wrong button or puts a bomb under the wrong castle, I would give us five more years at worst, twelve at best. What is triggering it is the crisis of reduced expectations. All over the world people are suddenly coming to realize that their children and grandchildren are going to have it worse than they did, that the trend line is down. So they want to blame somebody. They want to hoot and holler in the streets and burn something down."

"Whose side are you on?"

"I'm one of the scufflers. Cut and paste. Fix the world with paper clips and rubber bands."

"Are yo*u trying* to depress me, old buddy?"

"On Pearl Harbor Day?"

"So it is."

"And with each passing year it is going to seem ever more quaint, the little tin airplanes bombing the sleepy iron giants."

"There you go again."

He yawned and I noticed again how worn he looked. The international conference had been held in Zurich. There had been high hopes—the newspapers said—for a solution to the currency problems, but as it went on and on and on, interest could not be sustained, nor could hope.

"How was the trip back, Meyer?"

"I was too sound asleep to notice."

"Did you all just sit around and read papers to each other?"

"There was some of that. Yes. But most of it was workshop, computer analysis. Feed all the known, unchangeable factors into the program, and then add the ones that can be changed, predicating interdependence, making the variations according to a pattern, and analyzing the shape of the world that emerges, each one a computer model. Very bright young specialists assisted. We came out all too close to the doom anticipated by the Club of Rome, no matter how we switched the data around. It comes down to this, Travis—there are too many mouths to feed. One million three hundred thousand more every week! And of all the people who have ever been alive on Earth, more than half are living right now. We are gnawing the planet bare, and technology can't keep pace with need."

I had never seen him more serious, or more depressed. I fixed him a fresh drink when Gretel arrived. I met her, and after the welcome kiss, she looked over my shoulder and gave a whoop of surprise and pleasure at seeing Meyer. She thrust me aside and ran into his delighted bear hug. Then she held him off at arm's length and tilted her head to give him her brown-eyed measuring stare.

"You look *awful!*" she said. "You look like you just got out of jail."

"Fairly good guess. And you look fantastic, Gretel."

"It goes with the job. I got sort of sloppy living on this barge, eating too much and drinking too much. Today I jogged with four sets of fatties. I must have done seven miles. I've got the greatest new job."

"Travis was telling me about it."

"You'll have to come out and let me show you around." Quite suddenly the enthusiasm had faded out of her voice. I couldn't imagine why. She gave me a quick look and looked away, and went to the galley to fix herself one of her vegetable juice cock-tails.

I followed her and said, "Is something wrong out there?"

"No. Of course not."

"Hey, Grets. This here is me. Asking."

"I hear you asking. I think I might fall right off the wagon right now. I'm down to where I can spare a few pounds. Straight Boodles and rocks, okay?"

"When you come down off it, you come down a way."

She leaned against a storage locker as I fixed her drink. I looked at her, a great lithe woman who, on tiptoe, could almost look me in the eye. Thick brown sun-streaked hair, dark brown eyes, firm jaw, broad mouth, high-bridged imperious nose. A woman of passion, intensity, good humor, mocking grace, and a very irritating and compelling need for total—or almost total—independence. During all the lazy weeks aboard *The Busted Flush* when, after the death of her brother in Timber Bay, I had brought her all the way around the peninsula to Fort Lauderdale, we had arrived at last at a relationship she had decided did not threaten her freedom. She was a hearty and sensuous woman, and for a long time she was suspicious and reluctant in lovemaking, apparently feeling that my increasing knowledge of her body's resources, its needs and rhythms and special stimuli, was somehow an exercise in ownership. But after she decided to accept completely, she became herself—forthright, evocative, and deliciously bawdy when the mood was upon her.

After she took a sip of her drink I put fingertips under her chin, tilted it up, kissed her gently on the lips, and then said, "Whatever it is, I would like to know. Okay? Like management trying to slip up on your blind side?"

She grinned. *"That* I can handle, McGee. What makes you think there's a blind side?"

"If there isn't, what are you doing *here?*"

She frowned into her drink. "I think I'll tell both of you. I think I could use more than one opinion."

We went back in and she sat next to Meyer on the yellow davenport. "What it is," she said, "I think something other than what is supposed to be going on out there, is going on out there."

"Bonnie Brae is a front for something else?" I asked.

"Not really that," she said. "I mean, it's pretty big and elaborate. Mr. Ladwigg and Mr. Broffski borrowed a fantastic amount of money to buy the land. It's twelve hundred and eighty acres. There was a big stone-and-cypress house on it, and outbuildings. It was called the Cattrell place and was empty for years while the estate was being settled. They put a half-million dollars into renovating the house and some of the other buildings. And they put in roads and a sewage-treatment plant, water

17

supply, and all that. And they fixed the old airstrip near the barns. They are digging lakes, and building and selling houses, and selling building sites. We can accommodate twenty-four fatties in the main house at one time, feed them from the diet kitchen, and keep them busy. They pay twelve hundred a week, and there's a waiting list. And there's a waiting list for membership in the tennis club too. I mean, without knowing all the financial details, I'd say it's going very well. Mr. Ladwigg and Mr. Broffski have both built houses for themselves in the best part of the development, where the lots have to be two acres each, and Mr. Morse Slater, the manager, has a new house near theirs. There are twenty-five or thirty new houses occupied, and room for an awful lot more, of course. There are some staff quarters in the back of the main house, because it is sort of like a small hotel, or hospital. There is a nice flavor. I mean it's a good place to work. We have some laughs. People get along." Her voice trailed off and she sipped and frowned.

"And now something doesn't seem right?" Meyer asked, prompting her.

She smiled and leaned back. "Maybe I was lied to for too many years. Husband Billy was a world-champion-class liar. Brother John wasn't exactly clumsy at it."

"What's my rating?" I asked.

"All the returns aren't in. What I'm saying, maybe I get suspicious when there's no real need."

"We've got the whole evening, my dear," Meyer said. "If we're all patient, you'll probably get to the point sooner or later."

"I guess I'm dragging my feet because it sounds so weird I hate to mention it. Last week I had a batch of fatties down by the barns in the middle of the morning, making them do exercises, when a pretty little blue airplane landed on our strip. When I went back to the office, I asked Mr. Slater who had come in and he said that it was somebody to see Mr. Ladwigg, he didn't know what about. I asked because sometimes a buyer flies in, and when they buy something, it means more paperwork for me. Now we come to the coincidence part. I woke up real early the next morning. It was brisk and clear. The model house I'm living in is about a half mile from the office. A couple of days before, I lost a pin I like very much while leading a group jogging. So I put on a heavy sweater and went out to retrace our route, thinking maybe I could find it in the grass. I was over by the airstrip, searching near a patch of palmetto, when I heard a motor. For a moment I thought it was a plane, and then I stepped out almost into the path of Herman Ladwigg's Toyota, going cross-country. It's like a Land Rover, tall and open, with winches and things, and huge tires. It's white with red trim. Mr. Ladwigg was driving, and it startled him as much as it did me, I guess. I dodged back, and I was on the passenger side of it as it went by. So the face of the man riding with Mr. Ladwigg was not more than a yard away from me. I saw him very very clearly. And I knew in that split second I had seen him before. He looked right at me, and I saw the flicker of his recognition. He knew me too. But I couldn't remember where or when. All I could remember was that it had been an unpleasant experience."

"You can describe him?"

"Oh, sure. Big, but not fat. Big-boned. About forty, maybe a little less. Kind of a round face, with all his features sort of small and centered in the middle of all that face. Wispy blond hair cut quite short. No visible eyebrows or eyelashes. Lots and lots of pits and craters in his cheeks, from terrible acne when he was young. Little mouth, little pale eyes, girlish little nose. He was wearing a khaki jacket over a white turtleneck. He was holding onto the side of the passenger door because of the rough ride. His hands are very big and . . . well, brutal-looking."

Meyer said, "It doesn't sound as if there could be two like that. But it's possible, of course. Maybe his change of expression was not recognition, but surprise at seeing somebody pop up like that."

"No. He knew me. Because I remembered two nights ago, in the middle of the night, where I'd seen him. As soon as I remembered, I knew it was the same man. Five years ago Billy's sister, my kid

20

sister-in-law, Mitsy, disappeared. The family was frantic. She'd been in school up near San Francisco. She had just taken her things and gone away. Billy got time off from work and went up to San Francisco and nosed around and found out she had been hanging around with some kids who were connected with a religion called . . . damn! It will come to me."

"The Unification Church, the Moonies?" Meyer asked. She shook her head. "Hare Krishna? Scientology? Children of God? The Jesus People? The Church of Armageddon?"

She stopped him and said, "That's close, that last one. It's like Apocalypse. Wait a minute. Apocrypha! The Church of the Apocrypha."

"Very *interesting!*" Meyer said

"What's an apocrypha?" I asked.

"It's plural," he said. "Fourteen books or chapters which are sort of an appendix to the Old Testament and are not acceptable to the establishment. Seldom printed. They are bloody, merciless, and, some say, divinely inspired. Authorship unsubstantiated. I suspect that a religion based upon them would be . . . severe indeed."

"A postcard finally came from Mitsy," Gretel said. "It was mailed from Ukiah, California. It was to her mother, father, her two brothers, and me. All it said was, 'Remember that I will always love you, but I will never see you again in this life.' You can imagine how that hit us all. Mitsy was such a . . .

such a *merry* little gal. Pretty and bouncy and popular. Your standard cheerleader type. No steady
boyfriend. She wanted to be a social worker and
work with handicapped children.

"Anyway, her father hired an investigator, and
he located an encampment of the Church of the
Apocrypha about twenty miles southwest of Ukiah,
off in the woods. He had tried to get in to find out
if Mitsy was there, but he couldn't learn a thing.
Just about that time, her father—my father-in-
law—had a stroke, a severe one. His right side was
totally paralyzed, and he couldn't speak or understand what anyone said. He died of pneumonia
about four months later. Billy's younger brother
was working in Iran. So when we could, Billy and I
drove up to the encampment, using the map the investigator had marked.

"There were little winding roads, and finally we
came to the private, no-trespassing signs he had
told us about, and the wire gate across the road. A
young boy came out of a lean-to. He wore a dirty
white smock and he was trying to grow a beard. We
said we wanted to visit Miriam Howard, Mitsy
Howard. He nodded and walked away up the curving road beyond the wire gate, and out of sight. We
waited and waited and waited. Billy got very angry.
I had to keep talking him out of going over the
gate. It was over an hour before that man came
down the road. That *same man*. He was five years
younger, of course. He wore a white tunic with a

Chinese collar, and white trousers tucked into shiny black boots. He came right to the high fence and looked us over very carefully. He completely ignored the angry questions Billy was shouting at him.

"Finally he spoke to us. There was so little movement of his lips it was as if he were a ventriloquist. He had a soft little voice. 'I am Brother Titus. I am an elder of the Church of the Apocrypha. You are inquiring about someone we now know as Sister Aquila. She has asked me to tell you that she is quite happy here and she does not wish to see you or anyone from her previous life.'

"Billy demanded to see her. He swore at Titus. It had no effect. He said it wasn't possible, not now, not ever. She was happy in her new life, he said. Billy said he was going to see his sister Mitsy, and if it took a court order for a conservatorship, he would get it. He'd gotten that information from the investigator.

"Brother Titus thought for a little while and told us to wait. In twenty minutes a little crowd of them, about nine or ten, came down to the gate. We didn't see Brother Titus again. The people ranged in age from, I would guess, sixteen to twenty-five. Three or four girls, and the rest boys. At first we thought they had come without Mitsy, and then we recognized her. It was a shock. She had become such a worn, skinny, subdued little thing. She wore a dirty white smock and she had some kind of serious rash on her face and throat and arms. They looked badly chapped. The smock was too big for her. All of them had exactly the same look. It's hard to describe. Sort of bland and smug and glassy.

"They stood very close to her as she stood at the gate. She said, 'Hello, Billy. Hello, Gretel. I don't know how you found me, but I'm sorry you did.' Billy said, 'What have they *done* to you, Mitsy?' She said, 'My name is Sister Aquila now. They have made me very happy. I am full of peace and happiness and the love of God. Please don't ever try to find me again. Tell Mama and Papa I'm happy here, happier than I've ever been before.' Billy said, 'You better come home. Pop has had a very bad stroke. Things are in terrible shape. We all need you.' She didn't turn a hair. She looked at him with that contented half smile and said, 'All of that is in my previous life. It has nothing to do with me now. My life is here. Go away, please. God bless you.' They all turned and went up the hill together, so close together they made each other stumble from time to time. They all had exactly that same *look*. It took the heart right out of Billy."

"Did you make another try?" Meyer asked.

"Billy did. He went up there several weeks later, but they told him she was gone. They said she had been 'called' to another place in the service of the Lord. If it wasn't for the stroke, maybe the family would have taken some kind of action through the courts, but money was scarce, and God knows Billy and I couldn't finance a court order and deprogramming her and all that. The brother came back from Iran about six months before Billy ran out on me. Carl, his name is. He couldn't understand why we couldn't get her away from those people. He wasn't here. He couldn't know how it was. He lives in Houston now, at least he did the last I heard, and their mother lives with him and his wife."

"So you saw Brother Titus here, last week?" I said.

"Definitely. He was so . . . so out of context, it took a while to remember where I'd seen him before. But I am positive. Trav, there's another thing that seems odd. After they went by me, they headed for the airstrip, and a little later the blue plane took off. I *saw* it take off and head west. When Mr. Ladwigg drove back home, he drove on the road. Why did he take Brother Titus on such a roundabout way? Was it because Titus didn't want to be seen by anybody?"

"Maybe he was showing him some land. Maybe the Church wants to set up an encampment here," I said.

"Where there isn't any available? That piece was sold months ago."

"To whom?" Meyer asked.

"To some kind of foreign syndicate, headquartered in Brussels. I was told they plan to put up a hotel-club where members can come for holidays in the States. They took twenty undeveloped acres over on our western boundary near the airstrip."

"For foreign members of the Church of the Apocrypha?" Meyer asked with a sweet smile.

"Oh, no!" Gretel looked horrified. "Mr. Ladwigg and Mr. Broffski and Mr. Slater would have fits. It can't be that, really. Could it, Travis? Could that creep . . ."

"Not at the price they're probably getting out there."

"Two hundred and twenty-five thousand. It was a special price because of no roads or water supply or sewer."

"Maybe Brother Titus left the Church," I suggested. "Maybe he's into real estate. That has the status of a religion in south Florida."

She didn't laugh. She was scowling. "I keep thinking of Mitsy. Her hands were grubby and her hair was caked with dirt. She had sores on her ankles. She looked exhausted. I am damn well going to find out exactly what that man is doing around there. And it can't be anything good."

"You two are well-matched," Meyer said. "You both have the same kind of compulsive curiosity. I will tell you what I tell Travis, my dear. Proceed with caution. The world is full of damp rocks, with some very strange creatures hiding under them."

"Herm Ladwigg is an old honey bear," she said. "He would not be involved in anything tricky or dirty. And if I can think of the right way to ask him, he'll tell me what's going on."

The next time we looked at Meyer, we found he had fallen asleep in the chair. He would bitterly resent our leaving him like that, so we stirred him awake. He said he was too tired to eat, and over Gretel's protests that she could stir up something in a hurry, he went clumping on back to his stubby old cabin cruiser moored just down the pier from my slip, the *John Maynard Keynes*, sighing in consternation at the state of all the money in the world.

We buttoned up *The Busted Flush*. Gretel kicked off her shoes and hung herself around my neck and grinned into my face and said, "Well . . . will it be before or after the crab-meat feast I am going to fix us?"

I gave it judicious thought. "How about a little of both?"

"How did I know you were going to say that?"

"Because I usually do."

"Shut up and deal," she whispered.

So the gusty winds of a Friday night in December came circling through the marina, grinding and tilting all the play boats and work boats around us, creaking the hulls against the fenders, clanking fittings against masts. While in the big bed in the master stateroom her narrowed eyes glinted in faint reflected light, my hands found the well-known slopes and lifts and hollows of her warmth and agility. We played the games of delay and anticipation, of teasing and waiting, until we went past the boundaries of willed restraint and came in a mounting rush that seemed to seek an even greater closeness than the paired loins could provide. And then subsided, with the outdoor wind making breathing sounds against the superstructure of the old barge-type houseboat, and the faint swing and dip of the hull seeming to echo, in a slower pace, the lovemaking just ended. With neither of us knowing or guessing that it was the very last night. With neither of us able to endure that knowledge had we been told.

2

Because Gretel had too many jobs at Bonnie Brae, she went back out Saturday morning to catch up on her desk work, driving off in the little Honda Civic I had helped her find and buy. It had belonged to a hairdresser at Pier 66 who had decided to marry her friend and go live in Saudi Arabia. It was pink, with a special muffler.

She planned to come in again early Saturday evening and stay until Monday morning. It was a bright breezy day. My two best Finor reels were overdue for cleaning and oiling, and I had the first one all apart when Grets phoned me from work.

Her voice was hushed. "Darling, there is one hell of a mess out here. Herm is dead."

"Herm?"

"Ladwigg. Mr. Ladwigg. One of the owners."

"Heart attack?"

"They don't know yet. He's been bicycling early in the morning lately, for exercise, riding around the new roads they put in. And they found him in the middle of the road, face down, next to the bicycle. He either blacked out and the fall killed him . . . they just don't know yet. He was forty-six. What I wanted to say, don't expect me tonight, huh? Catherine—Mrs. Ladwigg—is in shock. They gave her a sedative. I'm here at the Ladwigg house trying to get in touch with their son and daughter. The son is a lawyer in Anchorage and the daughter works for the U.S. Embassy in Helsinki, and I haven't got through to either of them yet. When I do, I'm going to stay here until one or both of them get here. There's nobody else to do it. Stan Broffski's wife is a total loss in a situation like this."

"Want me to come out and help you wait around?"

"That's nice of you, but no, thanks."

"Let me know when you think you'll be free, when you have an idea of the time."

"Sure. Bye, dear."

So I went back to my fish reels. It was just ten o'clock, Saturday morning, December 8. They were having their weekend in Helsinki and in Anchorage. No telling how long it would take to find either of them. In the meanwhile, poor Herm had succumbed to the age of the jock. The mystique of pushing yourself past your limits. The age of shin splints, sprung knees, and new hernias. An office-softened body in its middle years needs a long, long time to come around. Until a man can walk seven miles in two hours without blowing like a porpoise, without sweating gallons, without bumping his heart past 120, it is asinine to start jogging. Except for a few dreadful lapses which have not really gone on too long, I have stayed in shape all my life. Being in shape means knowing your body, how it feels, how it responds to this and to that, and when to stop. You develop a sixth sense about when to stop. It is not mysticism. It is brute labor, boring and demanding. Violent exercise is for children and knowledgeable jocks. Not for insurance adjustors and sales managers. They do not need to be in the shape they want to be, and could not sustain it if they could get there. Walking briskly no less than six hours a week will do it for them. The McGee System for earnest office people. I can push myself considerably further because I sense when I'm getting too close to the place where something is going to pop, rip, or split.

Meyer stopped by a little while after I'd finished the reels. He said he had slept fourteen hours and still felt tired. I told him about the trouble out at Bonnie Brae, and he agreed with me that Ladwigg had probably pushed himself beyond his ability. A fall onto asphalt paving from a ten-speed bike going twenty miles an hour can easily be fatal, especially without a helmet. I doubted Ladwigg would wear a crash helmet while cruising his own development in the early hours.

Gretel phoned again at half-past noon to say she had located the son in Alaska and told him the news, and he expected to be able to get to Lauderdale late this same night.

"You sound a little beat," I said.

"Do I? The phone has been driving me crazy. But I do feel sort of blah. As if I'm coming down with a bug."

"Can you get somebody to take over?"

"I'm trying."

"I think I'll come on out."

"I . . . I'll be glad to see you."

Meyer left. I locked up the *Flush,* went over to the parking area, and cranked up my ancient Rolls pickup, the electric-blue Miss Agnes. The replaced power plant yanked her along too fast for her tall antique dignity, like a dowager blown into an unwilling trot by a gale-force wind. I made a stop on Spangler and picked up a pair of quarter-pounders with cheese, on the assumption that Gretel wouldn't have had time for lunch either.

I went all the way over to the University Drive intersection and turned north past the new plazas and shopping centers, the caramel-colored condominiums, the undeveloped flatlands where the palmetto still grew, the clusters of wooden town houses with roofs cut into steep new architectural clichés to shed some unimaginable snow load. Bonnie Brae had marked their entrance with squat fat brick pillars on either side of their divided-lane driveway. It curved off to the right to the big parking area near the renovated Cattrell place now used as clubhouse, fat farm, and administration building. When the gusty wind slowed, there was heat in the sun. I could see people bobbing and trotting about over on the tennis courts.

I went into the foyer of the building, hoping to find somebody who would direct me to Ladwigg's new house. A man came out of a room at my right and walked up to me, hand out.

"Mr. McGee?" He was a boyish thirty-something, with apple cheeks, a bushy blond mustache, thinning blond hair carefully adjusted to hide the thinning, bow tie, gray tweed jacket with leather elbows. When I nodded he shook my hand heartily and said, "I'm Morse Slater. Maybe Gretel has mentioned me."

"The manager, yes." He had a bumbling kind of effusiveness about him, a shoe-clerk willingness to please, which was given the lie by the ice-blue eyes, intent, aware, measuring. I said, "What I want to know is how I find the—"

"Gretel told me to look out for you. I just took her up the Drive to the hospital. Got back minutes ago."

"What happened?"

"Some sort of bug, I think. She seemed to be in a half faint, and she felt so hot to the touch it frightened me. So I took her right to Emergency and signed her in. They took her temperature and checked her into the hospital and began tests. A Dr. Tower seemed to be the one giving the orders. We accepted financial responsibility, of course. All our people have insurance which . . . but you're not interested in that. Room one thirty-three."

I think he tried to say something else, but I was already on my way. The hospital was on the same side of University Drive, and a little more than a half mile away.

I managed to talk my way to the nurses' station and then down the corridor to the room where Gretel was. It was a two-bed room with an old woman asleep and snoring by the windows, with a curtain drawn between the two beds. I pulled a straight chair close beside Gretel and took her hand. It felt dry and hot.

"What's going on?" I asked her.

Her lips were swollen and cracked, and her brown hair was damp and matted. She moistened her lips and gave me a small wry smile. "It's one of those days," she said. "Oh, boy. I got up and busted my favorite coffee mug that you gave me. Herm Ladwigg died in the street. A bug gave me a hell of a sting in the back of the neck. Later on, when I began to feel dizzy, I fainted and fell and broke one of the big lamps in the Ladwigg house. And here I am. It's one of those days."

"What do they say is wrong?"

"They don't say. Fever of unknown origin. My ears are ringing so loud you should be able to hear them. I really feel weird."

"They're running tests, aren't they? They'll find out what you've got."

A little bit of a sallow blond nurse came hurrying in. She had a fifty-year-old face and a twenty-five-year-old body. She gave me a disapproving glance, took a temperature reading with an electronic gadget, then took blood pressure on the left arm, pursed her lips, came around and displaced me, and took the pressure on the other arm. She trotted out. I moved close. Gretel found my wrist with her hot dry hand and held tight. "Trav, I feel so hot. I'm burning up. I feel terrible, Trav. Terrible."

When I spoke to her again, she didn't answer. She seemed to be asleep, her eyes about one third open, breathing so rapidly and shallowly through her mouth, it scared me.

I went plunging out to find somebody and ran into a couple of orderlies pushing a stretcher. I asked them what was going on, and they said they were taking a patient named Gretel Howard to Intensive Care. Other than that, they knew nothing.

I followed along, after they had raised the bed and pulled her across onto the stretcher. They tried to keep me from getting into the elevator with her, but it didn't work. But they did stop me at the door to the Intensive Care area. I told a very large white-haired nurse that if somebody didn't come and tell me within ten minutes what was going on, I was coming through that door.

The doctor who came out said his name was Tower. Vance Tower. He led me over to some rattan chairs near a window and we sat down and he said, "I need some background here."

"What's the matter with her?"

He had taken a little Pearlcorder out of his pocket and put it into dictation mode. "Name, address, and occupation, please," he said, and held it up between us. They make you play their game their way, and if you want a lot of delays, just refuse to go along. Travis McGee. Slip F-18, Bahia Mar Marina. Salvage Consultant.

"Relationship to patient?"

I hesitated, then said, "Common-law husband." After all, she had lived aboard the houseboat with me for a lot of weeks.

He was a dumpy-looking man, soft and pale and too heavy, going bald, short of breath, looking out of tired little brown eyes at me, showing no reaction at all to my answers.

"How can we contact her close relatives?"

"There aren't any. Parents and only brother are dead. She is divorced from her first husband. No children. I think there may be some distant kin, second cousins and so on, but I would have no idea how to reach them."

"Where has she been lately? Geographically, that is."

"Lately? Up until May she was living in Timber Bay over on the west coast. Then we came around to Lauderdale aboard my houseboat. We took our time. Got here in early August. She lived aboard and then moved to one of the model houses at Bonnie Brae to be closer to her work. A temporary arrangement."

"Did she go out of the country at any time since last May?"

"No."

"Has she been in swamp country?"

"No. Why?"

"Do you know if any of the people she has been associated with have been taken seriously ill, quite suddenly?"

"I don't know if this is what you mean, but one of the owners of Bonnie Brae fell off his bicycle this morning and—"

"I know about that. I mean an illness like hers, characterized by extremely high temperatures, sporadic delirium, cardiac arrhythmia, and fading blood pressure."

"I can't think of anyone we know who's been sick lately. What's wrong with her?"

"I've ordered every lab test I can think of. I don't approve of the shotgun approach to antibiotics, but I'm giving her a wide range of those. If we can't knock that fever down any other way, I'm going to try packing her in ice." He sighed heavily. "The big problem with treating something when you don't know what it is, you can make diagnosis all that more difficult."

"Can I see her?"

He thought it over, then nodded. "They'll be busy in there. You can see her five minutes out of every hour. I'll approve that. It won't be pleasant for you, and I doubt if she'll know you're there."

A nurse came out and motioned to him, and he got up and plodded in, through the double doors. Man at work. A very tired man. But he was an empathetic man because, about ten minutes later, he beckoned to me and took me to her bedside. The rapid shallow breathing had eased. There was an I.V. rigged, dripping into the vein in her arm. Her cheeks seemed hollower than they had looked an hour before, in her room, her eyes more sunken.

He said in a low voice, "We knocked the fever down almost one degree. First sign of progress."

We walked out together and he said, "I'm making a full report of all our findings to Disease Control in Atlanta. Do you know anything about the red welt on the back of her neck?"

"She told me she was bitten by a bug this morning. She said it stung her."

"Symptoms bear no relation to anaphylactic shock. We've taken some tissue from the area. It's being packed in dry ice and flown to Atlanta, along with blood samples and so forth. Got more sophisticated analysis systems available up there. Paper chromatography. Thin-layer chromatology techniques."

The hours blurred. I went in as often as I could. Night and day inside hospitals are too much alike. Saturday night. Sunday. Sunday night. She kept changing, little by little, going further away from me. They did a tracheotomy, and from then on a machine was doing her breathing for her, pumping her chest up and down. When I bent close to her to touch my lips to her dank forehead, I could detect the faint sour smell of mortal illness. At one point, early in the vigil, I went out to the car and made the mistake of trying to eat one of the clammy hamburgers and was sick on the asphalt.

Meyer came out, bringing a change of clothes and my toilet kit. A nurse found me a towel and took me to a place where I could shower and scrape the pale stubble off my tired brown jaws.

Somebody forgot to stop me and tell me. I went in a little after eleven on Monday night, and she was gone. The bed was empty. The equipment had been moved away.

"Where is she?" I roared, and they came running toward me, hushing me, ushering me toward the door.

A big black nurse, big as a tight end, had been answering questions for me during other visits during that shift. She took hold of my shoulders and gave me a shake. "Easy now! Easy now!" she said in a husky whisper. "It's better we lost her."

"Better than what?"

"Hush now. You hush down. A temperature like that, for so long, it cooked her brain. She would have been a vegetable. Terrible thing, a strong young woman like that." She had led me out into the corridor. "Who you got to come get you?"

"I'll manage." I tried to smile. The tears were running down my face. No sobs. No shudders. Just eyes running. "Where is she now?"

"They're doing an autopsy."

"Who said they could!"

"It's a law, Mr. McGee. When the cause of death is unknown, they have to. There's no way anybody can stop them, and that's a good law. Whatever is killing people, we have to find it out."

"What finally happened? There was that machine . . ."

She shrugged. "Total kidney failure, and then the heart gave out right about the same time." She shook her head. Her eyes were shining with unshed tears. "I don't know. We get so many old ones here.

Not young strong women like her. Whatever it was, it came and wore her right down to nothing. It took the life right out of her. It ate her up, like it was some hungry thing." She caught herself. "Sorry. I talk too much. Listen, if you're the only one she had, what you've got to do now, you've got to make the arrangements. She's got to have a burial."

I walked on out of their hospital, snuffling from time to time, marveling that I could walk with so little thought and effort. Long strides, heels thudding against the tile floor, hand lifting without conscious command to flatten against the push plate on the big glass door, push and let me out into the chill night, spangled with stars that were faint above the security lights of the parking area. I walked to the tall dark shape of Miss Agnes, my ancient Rolls, and leaned against one of her high front fenders, my arms folded, ankles crossed, eyes running again.

Cessation. Ending. A stopping of her. I heard the night sounds of country and city. Yawk of a night bird nearby. Faraway eerie pulsing of siren. Whispering drone of light traffic on University Drive, lights in moving patterns. Grinding whine of trucks moving fast, a mile or so away. Random night wind clattering palm fronds. This was the world, bustling its way on through its allotted four billion more years of time, carrying its four billion souls gracelessly onward. A lot of them had stopped

John D. MacDonald

tonight, some in blood and terror. I tried to comprehend the enormity—the obscenity—of the fact that Gretel Howard had been one of them, just as dead as the teenagers who impacted a tree at a hundred and ten miles an hour near Tulsa, the flying dentist who didn't see the power lines, the Muslim children dead by fire in Bangladesh, the three hundred elderly in Florida who would not make it through the night in their nursing-home beds.

I could not fit my mind around the realization of finality. There seemed to be more that would happen for the two of us, more of life to be consumed and completed. My body knew with a dreadful precision all the contours of her, the shapes and fittings, the sighs and turnings, gasps and pressures.

I sought refuge in a child's dreaming. They had spirited her away, mended her, and would soon spring the great surprise upon me. She would come running, laughing, half crying, saying, "Darling, we were just fooling you a little. That's all. Did we scare you too much? I'm sorry, Trav, dear. So sorry. Take me home."

And on the way home she would explain to me how she had outwitted the green ripper. I had read once about a little kid who had overheard some adult conversation and afterward, in the night, had terrible nightmares. He kept telling his people he dreamed about the green ripper coming to get him. They finally figured out that he had heard talk about the grim reaper. I had told Grets about it, and it had found its way into our personal language. It was not possible that the green ripper had gotten her.

Not possible.

3

Meyer took care of practically everything. I
couldn't have managed. I was too listless and too
depressed. We both remembered that after her
brother's death at Timber Bay, Gretel said she preferred cremation, just as he had. Cremation and
maybe a small nondenominational memorial service
for close friends. Not many people had attended
John Tuckerman's memorial service in Timber
Bay. He had been too closely associated with Hub-
bard Lawless, the man who had taken all the
money and tried to run.

I did not think there would be many people who
would want to come to Gretel's memorial service.
Meyer arranged it at a small chapel up beyond

South Beach Park, at eleven in the morning on Saturday, ten days before Christmas.

Ten or so people came in from Bonnie Brae. And a lot of people from the Bahia Mar area. Meyer calls it a subculture, the permanents. The great waves of tourists and boat people flood the area and recede, leaving the same old faces, most of them, year after year. I did not see all of them come in. When it was over and we walked out into December sunshine, they were there, moving toward me to touch, to shake hands, to kiss, to say some fumbly words: We're sorry. That's what it was about. Together we form a village. And share the trouble as much as we can. Take as much of it upon ourselves as is possible, and we know it is not very much. Okay?

There was Skeeter, and there were Gabe and Doris Marchman—Gabe's metal crutches glinting in the sun. From charter-boat row there were Billy Maxwell, Lew and Sandy, Barney and Babs, Roxy and his nephews. There was the Alabama Tiger, and Junebug was with him, looking strangely subdued. Raul and Nita Tenero were there, up from Miami, with Merrimay Lane. There were Irv Deibert and Johnny Dow, and Chookie and Arthur Wilkinson, back together again. And there were others, from the hotel and the shops, the boatyards and the tethered fleet.

My village and my people. They seemed to know what I needed most, a sense of place, the feeling of belonging to some kind of resilient society. A man can play the game of being the loner, moving unscathed through an indifferent world, toughened by the diminished expectations of his place and time. I spoke to them, thanked them, managing to keep myself together. As I did so, I thought of the ones who weren't there any more. Lois, of course. Puss Killian. Mike Gibson, of the world before I came to the marina. Nora Gardino. Barni Baker, who went down with her 727 into the swamp short of the airfield. Too damn many of them. I could just barely stand losing them, but I couldn't handle having Gretel gone too. She was destined to be a part of the life that would come after the marina. But she was gone and I was fixed there, embedded in time, embedded in a life I had in some curious way outgrown. I was an artifact, genus boat bum, a pale-eyed, shambling, gangling, knuckly man, without enough unscarred hide left to make a decent lampshade. Watchful appraiser of the sandy-rumped beach ladies. Creaking knight errant, yawning at the thought of the next dragon. They don't make grails the way they used to. She had deserted me here, left me in this now unbreakable mold, this half-farcical image, trapped me in my solitary, fussy, bachelor hang-ups from now until they turned me off too. I shook hands, I hugged and was hugged, and I tried to smile into reddened eyes, and they left, slowly, car doors chunking, driving away from the sunlit ceremony of farewell to my girl.

I had parked Miss Agnes two blocks away. An electric-blue Rolls hand-hewn into a pickup truck seemed too conspicuous and frivolous for a memorial service for my dead.

After we got in and I waited for the chance to move out from the curb, Meyer said, "Did it go all right? Did he pick the right things to read?"

"It was fine."

"I tried to ask you ahead of time, but I couldn't seem to get through."

"It was fine."

I thought of the fine running we had done, Gretel and I, on the beach near the shack where her brother was living. I thought of making love with her on the sun deck at dusk, in a hard warm summer rain. I had never really told her how much it all meant. There was going to be plenty of time for that. All the rest of her life. I could make a list of the things we were going to talk about someday. When we had the time.

"Good turnout," Meyer said.

"For God's sake!"

"So I'll keep my mouth shut."

"Fine."

I wanted to apologize, but couldn't find the right way to begin, and so the rest of the ride was silent. He sat beside me like a gloomy bear. I knew his feelings weren't hurt. He was sad because I had lost Gretel, and because we had lost Gretel.

"I picked out an urn," he said, as we pulled into

the parking place. "Nothing ornate. Bronze, though. Seventy-two something, including tax. He wrapped it up in a box and brown paper, ready for mailing."

"I might take it out there."

"I told him you might do that," he said. "I've got the box at my place. I'll bring it over. Unless you'd like to have me go on out there with you."

"I'll let you know, Meyer. Keep it for now. And thanks."

He headed over to the newsstand to see if his copy of *Barron's* had come in, and I walked back to *The Busted Flush*, anxious to get out of the suit and get the necktie off. And anxious to see how much Boodles gin I could fit into a king-size old-fashioned glass.

Two men had boarded my houseboat. They were on my little back porch aft the lounge, one sitting on a folding stool, the other leaning against the rail. They were of a size and age, middle height, middle forties, a tailored three-piece gray suit, with white shirt, black shoes, blue necktie with a white figure; a tailored three-piece chocolate-brown suit, with white shirt, brown shoes, tan necktie with a small figure. Gray Suit wore a gray tweed snapbrim hat, and Brown Suit wore a dark brown hound's-tooth tweed hat. Soft jowls, pale faces, horn-rim glasses on one, metal-rim glasses on the other. One stood up and the other pushed off from the rail as I came aboard.

The Green Ripper

"Mr. McGee?" said Gray Suit.

The brain is a swift and subtle computer. I have perhaps become more sensitive to the clues which exist in mannerisms, stance, expression, hand gestures, and dress than most people. If you are in a line of work where a bad guess can give you a pair of broken elbows, you tend to become a quick study.

They were not going to try to sell me anything. They did not have the twinkle, the up-front affability. They were not here to enforce one of the idiot rules of a bureaucracy that grows like high-speed cancer. They did not have that look of fatuous satisfaction and autocratic, patronizing indifference of fellows who come to tell you that you forgot to file Form Z-2324, as amended. Or to tell you that you can't cut down your pine tree without enlisting the services of an approved, accredited, licensed tree surgeon.

They looked important. As if they had come to buy the marina and put up a research institute. Lawyers? Executives? They were not very fit. They moved heavily. They looked out of place aboard my houseboat, as if it was a little closer to the outdoor life than they cared to be.

"I am not exactly cheered up by people coming aboard without being asked," I said.

"Forgive the intrusion, please," Gray Suit said. He had been the one sitting. "I am not familiar with marine protocol, Mr. McGee. We were told this is your houseboat, and we have been waiting for you. My name is Toomey. This is Mr. Kline."

"I am not in the mood for visitors or transactions or conversation about anything."

"We are anxious to talk to you," Kline said. He had picked up a dispatch case I had not noticed before. It matched his suit color. "I think it would all go more smoothly if you did not put us in the position where we would have to insist."

I studied him. "You are telling me that if you have to insist, you have the leverage to make it stick?"

"We do indeed," said Toomey. "And we would rather not."

So I unlocked and we went into the lounge. I have played respectable poker over the years. I won my houseboat on a broken flush, four pink ones up and a stranger down. I can sense when a bluff is a bluff is a bluff. They had the leverage, and the clothes and manner to go with it.

Before I invited them to sit down while I changed, I asked to see credentials. They looked vaguely like passports, small with the dark blue cover and great seal of the U. S. of A. Inside were the color ID pictures, the thumbprint, and the name of an agency I had never heard of before.

"We do not usually go out into the field," Toomey said. "We have access to another agency for investigative matters. But after a conference with our superior, it was suggested that we take a firsthand look."

"At what?"

"Excuse me. I thought you'd guessed."

"Guessed what?"

"We want to ask you what you know about Gretel Tuckerman Howard."

"I just came back from her memorial service."

"We know that," Kline said.

"Sit down. I'll be back in a minute."

I took my time changing into old flannel slacks, Mexican sandals, and an old wool shirt. There was a small chill spot at the nape of my neck. A warning of some kind.

They had moved a couple of chairs close to the coffee table. Kline had a little Sony TC-150 opened up, and he was breaking the seal on a new cassette. "I hope you won't mind that I tape this."

"Go right ahead."

He put the tape in, put it on Record and counted to ten, rewound, played it back, rewound again, and said, "December fifteenth, one ten P.M., initial interview by Toomey and Kline with Travis McGee aboard his houseboat moored at Slip F-Eighteen, Bahia Mar Marina, Fort Lauderdale, Florida."

Toomey took over. "Please describe your relationship to the decedent. Wait. Excuse me. Where and when did you meet her?"

"Earlier this year. May. At a beach shack where her brother was living. John Tuckerman. South of

Timber Bay, over on the west coast of Florida. The northwest coast. Her brother died a little while later. I went with Gretel when she flew out to California to have his ashes buried in a little cemetery in Petaluma. We flew back to Timber Bay and, sometime in June, we left Timber Bay in this houseboat and came down around the peninsula and back up here to Lauderdale. We made it a leisurely trip. We got here in August. She lived aboard until she located the job at Bonnie Brae in early November and moved out there, to one of the model houses."

With great delicacy Toomey asked, "Would you say that you and she had a . . . a significant relationship?"

"I didn't care what rules we went by, as long as we both agreed that it would be a permanent thing. Why do you have to know stuff like this?"

"We want to know whether the relationship was such that she would confide in you."

"Confide what?"

"Let us just say details of her workday, her life out there. That sort of thing."

"Are you looking into something fishy at Bonnie Brae?"

"Did Mrs. Howard say something fishy is going on at Bonnie Brae?"

"No. No, she didn't. I mean, she called up last Saturday morning before she got sick, to tell me about one of the owners, Mr. Ladwigg, dying in an accidental fall on his bicycle, if that's what you mean."

Kline took over. "Let me set up a hypothesis, Mr. McGee, and see if that helps. Suppose Mrs. Howard, in the course of her employment out there, learned that something curious was going on. Say that part of the operation was a cover for something else, like gambling or smuggling or something of that nature. Would she have confided in you?"

"Of course."

"Would she have confided something like that to anyone other than you? Or as well as you?"

"I can't see that happening."

"And she talked to you about her work?"

"Certainly. About her exercise classes of fatties, and the tennis lessons she was giving to children, and the forms she had to complete on each sale of land, houses, and so forth. She liked her work."

The two men looked at each other, and Kline reached over and punched the key to turn off the recorder. Toomey said, "We do appreciate your cooperation, Mr. McGee."

"Wouldn't you say you owe me some kind of explanation . . . why you are interested in Gretel Howard?"

Toomey smiled sadly. "I wish we could. I really wish we could. There was a possibility she could have acquired some information which would have been useful to us. Unfortunately she became ill before we had a chance to speak with her."

"If I happen to remember something later on, how do I get in touch with you?" I asked. "I'm pretty upset right now and I'm not thinking too clearly."

Kline tore a sheet out of a small spiral notebook and wrote a number on it: (202) 661-7007. I thanked him. They put the recorder away in the dispatch case, smiled politely, put on their hats, and marched off, down my little gangplank and off toward the parking area, in step, arms swinging in unison.

Three minutes later Sue Sampson arrived, bearing a casserole of hot beef stew. She apologized for having to miss the service and took off just as Meyer arrived.

I made the delayed drinks. Meyer put the stew over low heat while we sat and he listened to the saga of Toomey and Kline.

"All right," he said, "so you sidestepped. You left out Brother Titus and the blue airplane and the twenty-acre sale to a syndicate in Brussels. But you make them sound very authentic."

"While they were boring in, I was deciding several things. First, that I am not in very good emotional shape to spar with anybody about anything. Second, that I could get in touch with them later. Third, that they were almost too perfect. Too cold and clean. They had no regional accent that I could detect. They said they did not usually go out into the field. That implied some importance to talking to me. But it never came off as important. They wanted some hearsay about what might be going on at Bonnie Brae. Colloquial American pronunciation, but a stilted kind of sentence structure. Almost like you when you are at your most professorial."

"Didactic is a better word. The tendency to lecture others."

"Kline made those little continental crossbars on the sevens in the phone number. See?"

"But that came after you had decided to hold off."

"Before that, their pants were too long. Long enough almost to step on the back of the cuffs. Like Kissinger. The necktie knots were wrong. Frenchmen tie them that way. When Kline cleaned his glasses and held them up to the light, I looked through them too, and I saw no distortion."

"So the glasses were a very minor correction. So both of them have lived and worked abroad. So they spoke another language before they learned English."

"I know. I know. But, dammit, it seemed like such an invasion of my personal privacy to have strangers here asking me to talk about Gretel. I am not ready to talk about Gretel to anybody. I am not impressed by official credentials. Nor by Mr. Robert A. Toomey or Mr. Richard E. Kline, on the staff of the Select Committee on Special Resources in the Senate Office Building."

"Are you sure you remember that accurately?"

"I'm sure."

Meyer wrote it down on Kline's piece of paper. "No great problem to check it out on Monday, if you'd like."

"I'd like."

"Ready for stew?"

"Right after the next drink. If it all checks out, I'll forget my paranoia and phone them and tell all."

"And what if it doesn't check out? What if your instincts were accurate?"

"Then I'm going to have to try to figure out what they were really after. The cover story was very elaborate. I wouldn't think they'd have gone to all that trouble just for me. I would be incidental to something more important to them, or to someone."

I had one drink more than I needed. Meyer dished out the stew. I managed almost half of what he served me. He wanted to clean up, but I shooed him out, sent him home.

After I washed the dishes, I locked up and went over the pedestrian bridge to the beach. A high gray overcast had moved in, pushed by a cool fitful breeze off the sea. I had put on good shoes for walking, and I headed north on packed damp sand, lunging along, carrying with me my sorrow, my mild headache, my sour stomach, and the dull pain in my right thigh which cold and damp will cause. I plodded along the beach all the way up to Galt

Ocean Mile, and from there on I alternated between the beach and A-1-A, depending on obstacles. The cold and the oncoming dusk had emptied the beaches. The glassy facades of the condominiums glittered down at me.

I pushed hard, but even so it had been dark a long time when I crossed back over to the mainland on the Atlantic Boulevard bridge at Pompano Beach. I walked the seven short blocks to North Federal Highway. They were promoting Christmas carols at the big shopping center, pumping them out into the night wind. Jangle bells. And the silent stars go by.

When I found a saloon, I had a small draft beer and phoned a cab. One Oscar Lopez arrived in a rattle-bang rig that smelled strongly of cigar and faintly of vomit. He was dubious about the length of the trip compared with the appearance of the passenger, and I had to show him that I had money. Though he played loud rock and drove badly, he did not have to be told to turn east at Sunrise. He let me off at the marina. I walked to my houseboat, let myself in. It was empty. I had gotten used to a certain amount of emptiness after she had moved way out there to Bonnie Brae. But it had been a conditional emptiness. She could and would return. But now it was a hollowness beyond belief. Even the promise of life and warmth had been drained out of that clumsy old hull. She was hollow, brittle, tacky, and old, sighing in a night wind, smelling faintly of onion, unwilling to admit that Gretel had ever lived here with me. My legs were leaden with fatigue. The small beer was caught in the back of my throat. Gretel was turned to ash and confined in bronze. The green ripper sailed by on the night wind, looking for more customers. I suggested, politely, that I would give him no big argument this time. But there were others with a higher priority tonight.

4

I got through Sunday—with a little help from my friends. It was a day of cold December rain. I uncrated and hooked up my new speakers. They had been delivered ten days ago. Once they were positioned and adjusted, I tied them down. I had been going to give the old ones to Gretel to give to a friend, but I couldn't remember the friend's name.

The new ones had a great big full rich sound for such small enclosures. They worked all day long. Big music and Bloody Marys. People came by and brought bottles and food and stayed for a time and left again. When it would begin to get too noisy, somebody would remember that too much merriment was probably in bad taste, and things would quiet down, but not for long. It was a party related to a wake.

At the bitter end of the day there was but one guest left aboard. I had heard about her but had never met her. She was the third or fourth wife of some old party from Long Island whose hundred-and-twenty-foot ocean-going yacht was moored at one of the big berths, with a permanent crew of five. The *Madrina,* meaning "godmother," a nice enough name for a ship. The *Madrina* had been at the marina for a month because her owner had a very bad stroke the day before they were to sail for Bermuda. I did not know who brought the wife aboard my vessel, or left her there with me. Smallish, dark-haired, and very nice to look upon, she was a creature of many subtle perfections. Named Anna. An accent I could not place. Some Portuguese, she said, and Chinese, and a lot of White Russian, born in Hong Kong, and with a degree in engineering from the University of Alabama.

Anna wore a woolly white jump suit with a turtleneck, a heavy-duty gold zipper all the way down the front of it, and some little marine flag signals embroidered over the pocket. At five of midnight, after the others had left, there we were. She was curled into a corner of my yellow sofa, brandy glass in hand, looking over at me out of dark eyes under dark brows under the wing of smooth jet hair across her forehead. She stared with a total focus of her attention, watchful as a cat. The white outfit fitted so closely no one with figure flaws could have managed it. I couldn't remember who had brought her into the group.

"We have very much the same kind of trouble, Travis," she said.

"We do?"

"They told me the day before yesterday, at the hospital, that Harvey won't live."

"I'm sorry to hear it."

"Just two short years. That's all we had."

"Yes. That's too bad."

"Any day now."

"Those things happen."

"I need advice about the *Madrina*."

"What kind of advice?"

"They told me you know all about boats."

"I don't know anything about ships. Over a hundred feet is a ship, unless it is a submarine, and then it's still a boat."

"Advice about selling it. If I should sell it here or have them take it back home. I don't trust Michael."

"Who is Michael?"

"He is the captain. Maybe if it is best to take it home to sell it, you could help me."

"A boat is a hole in the water into which you throw money. A ship is a bigger hole into which you throw more money. If you don't want it, move off it right now. Get rid of the crew and all perishables, cancel the telephone hookup, and turn it over to one of the brokers. There are good ones here."

"I really can't do that until after all that will and executor thing is taken care of."

"And he isn't even dead yet."

"The way you say that, you make me sound . . . terrible."

"Not intended."

"I didn't think it would be unreasonable, Travis, to suggest that we might help each other. And comfort each other." She added a slight arching of the back, for emphasis. A very subtle movement of her left hand indicated that I should come over and sit by her.

I stood up and said, "I'm dead, Anna. I'll walk you back around to the *Madrina*."

She tossed off the rest of the brandy, frowned, shrugged, and let me walk her home. She hung onto my forearm with both hands and contrived to bump a hip into me every now and again.

"What if I want to fire Michael and he won't let himself be fired by me?"

I was supposed to volunteer assistance. "Then you'll have to let the executor fire him, I guess."

"He's worked for Harvey for twenty-three years."

We stopped at the gangplank. She said, "Would you like to come aboard and look around?"

"Not really."

"You're not very gracious, are you?"

"Not very."

"Well . . . if you feel terribly lonely and want someone to talk to who . . . faces the same kind of sorrow, I'll be nearby. Okay?"

"Okay, Anna. Sure. 'Night."

I walked slowly home to *The Busted Flush.* There was a sour smell in the night air, like a broken drain. Anna was a very tidy little biscuit, with her old dark eyes set in that child's face. She exuded a tantalizing flavor of corruption, of secret, unspeakable experience. There had been times in my life when I would have been happy to help her pass the time until old Harv died and then talked her into letting me help her take the *Madrina* home, by way of a lot of nice islands.

But I had seen the crocodile tears bulging in her dark eyes when she had said, "Any day now." And I had seen the greed behind the tears, the impulse to break into laughter. Everything old Harv had is now mine, fella. All, all mine. During those past two years she had probably been dreadfully afraid that he would live forever.

When you see the ugliness behind the tears of another person, it makes you take a closer look at your own.

We are all at the mercy of the scriptwriters, directors, and actors in cinema and television. Man is a herd creature, social and imitative. We learn the outward manifestations of inner stress, patterning reaction to what we have learned. And because the visible ways we react are so often borrowed, we wonder about the truth of what is happening underneath. Do I *really* feel pain, grief, shock, loss?

It is as if we look inside and take a tentative rap at some bell that hangs in there. I had the horrid feeling that *maybe* my pain was tempered by some sick measure of relief, that I had escaped the trap of a permanent twoness.

Take a rap at that bell, dreading a possible flat, cracked, dissonant sound of self-pity, of a grubby selfishness.

But it rang true. It rang for her, for my lost girl. The loving and the losing were still larger than life. Than my life. The sound of the bell was almost unbearable. I was like a rat in a cage, subjected to supersonic experimentation. They run back and forth and roll at last onto their backs, chewing their paws bloody. I wanted to swim straight out into the sea. Or go visit Anna and help her into bed. Each was a form of drowning.

5

On Monday morning I awoke glum, got up glum, dressed glum. The sky was a bright pewter, a radiance that cast no shadow but made people squint and walk hunched over, as if searching for something. It would be windless and silent one moment, then a hard blast would come slamming past, picking up dust devils and scraps of paper before subsiding into stillness. At sea on a day like this I would have been laying a course to the nearest shelter and checking the fuel level to see how fast I dared go to get there. It is the kind of weather that makes people cross.

Meyer was cross when he arrived at eleven for reheated coffee.

"How are you?" he asked, peering at me.

"Peachy."

"I'm sorry. It is the standard question one asks. How did you get rid of little Anna?"

"Walked her back to her personal ship. What made you jump to the conclusion I got rid of her?"

"Not such a big jump. Why shouldn't you get rid of her? There'd be no reason to keep her around."

"Who brought her and dumped her on me?"

"Lili MacNair. And it wasn't her fault. She just couldn't get the Farmer woman to leave."

"Farmer?"

"Anna Farmer."

"Don't look so exasperated, Meyer. I never caught her last name. Is she worth talking about, even? And does it matter a damn one way or another what I do or don't do with my days or with my nights?"

"Aha!" he said. "Tragic figger of a man."

"Meyer, I know what you are trying to do, and I forgive you. But don't keep it up. Understand?"

He stared and finally nodded. "All right. I was out of line. A transparent, clumsy attempt to cheer the troops. What I came over for, aside from dispensing hollow cheer, was to complain about the bureaucracy. And to give you a conundrum to occupy your mind."

"A riddle?"

"Somewhat. I was on the phone at a reasonable morning hour, calling old friends in Washington.

There are a lot of offices up there. And strange titles. Deputy Director to the Assistant Director in charge of the Policy Committee on Administration. The phone directory is gigantic. I gave them the information and set them to scurrying about. I gave the same mission to three quite different people in three quite different departments, and then waited for the results. The last call came in fifteen minutes ago. That phone number they gave you is not an operating number. There is not now and never has been, at least in living memory, any Select Committee on Special Resources. The central register of all civil servants has no Robert A. Toomey, but it does have two Richard E. Klines. One is twenty-five and works for the Department of the Interior in Alaska. The other is sixty-one and based in Guam. Interesting?"

My head was too full of fragments, like a kaleidoscope, making its bright patterns of nonsense. I had decided that when they had visited me, my reaction had been paranoid.

"I don't know what to think, Meyer. Don't they have departments sort of hidden away, without public records and so forth?"

"So why give you a bad phone number?"

"Maybe you would like to try to make sense out of it."

"Too many parts missing," he said. He got up and roamed around the lounge, sighing audibly, pausing to look out the port, then resuming his circuit. "High-level inquiry," he said.

"What?"

"Excuse me. I'm talking to myself."

He roamed and muttered and finally sat down. He gave me a bright false smile. "It's all too melodramatic. There is but one way I can make the parts fit together, and it offends me."

"See if it offends me."

"It will more than offend, Travis. All right. Postulate X. X is an unknown force, group, movement, with unknown objectives. X is powerful and has high-priority objectives. Secrecy is imperative. Brother Titus represents the syndicate in Brussels, and he came down here from another part of the country to take a look at the land and make contact with Mr. Ladwigg. The odds against anyone seeing him and recognizing him are astronomical. But that is one way in which life is consistently quirky. It keeps serving up unlikely coincidences. Gretel told us her story about Brother Titus on December seventh. And she said she had seen him 'last week,' if I remember correctly. Not 'this week,' 'last week.' The last week in November. Brother Titus went back to X and reported being recognized. For some reason, this created a great danger to the high-priority objective. They had a week in which to plan and move. Their representatives were in the area by mid-week, perhaps, or earlier. On Saturday morning Ladwigg fell off his bike and died. Gretel was taken ill on Saturday. They are the only two, we can assume, who saw Titus face to face. Toomey and Kline came here Saturday to find out if Gretel told you about him. From what you told me of the questioning, they would have gotten the information from anyone less wary than you."

"What the hell are you trying to say?"

"I *told* you the reconstruction is so melodramatic it offends me. If you had told them all about Brother Titus, as related by Gretel, right now you might be in the hospital, fading fast."

I thought it over. I could not make it seem real. "Okay, why the charade? If what is going on is so important, why not just wait until dark, thump my skull, and let me go out on the tide?"

"They do not want to create curiosity. A man falls off his bike and dies. One of the young women who work for him falls ill and dies. The authorities can accept that as routine. But what if the woman's best friend should then die accidentally, or be taken ill in the same way?"

"The authorities would assume the friend caught it from her, whatever it was."

"But that would create a big flap. Gretel's illness and death were reported, you said, to the Center for Disease Control in Atlanta."

"By Dr. Tower."

"Having it turn out to be contagious would make headlines."

"Mental games are your specialty, Meyer. But it

does not amuse me one goddamn bit to have you making a lot of assumptions based on Gretel being murdered, poisoned somehow. For God's sake, you saw her that one time there! She was sick. She was terribly, terribly ill. Know what her last words were? 'I'm burning up. I feel terrible, Trav. Terrible.' Great last words to remember. Comforting. Dammit, she could have mentioned Titus to those people out there at Bonnie Brae. She could have asked about him. She could have asked the other partner, or Slater. And she could have told them about the fellow just the way she told us."

"The way she told us, remember, was to start by saying she thought there was something funny going on out there. And she would not be likely to bring that up with the people she was working for. Or with. And one good way to prove I am totally wrong is to find out if Broffski and Slater have been questioned, just as you were. I don't think that pair came here from out of town to talk to you alone."

I looked at him. "If I thought for one moment that somebody had . . . poisoned her . . ."

"I am not sitting here, Travis, trying to dream up a cheap plot line for a grade Z movie. You asked me to try to make sense out of it. I can make melodramatic sense out of it, *if* I make the assumption that both Gretel and Ladwigg were killed. If they weren't, the sense of it all eludes me."

"You're *serious!*"

"Enough to want to try to prove it out one way or the other."

"Where would you start?"

"By finding out if Broffski and Slater were questioned too."

So once again I drove out to Bonnie Brae. I could not have guessed how difficult it would be. Memories of her were of a painful clarity, a vividness in the back of the mind.

Slater, the manager, was out for lunch. Stanley Broffski was in his office. What did we wish to speak to him about? the woman asked. I said it involved some negotiations with Herman Ladwigg. She trotted off and soon reappeared, beckoning us in.

Broffski sat behind a big white desk covered with piles of correspondence and blueprints. He was plump to the point of bursting out of his sport shirt. He had black hair combed across his forehead and a Groucho mustache. He had an air of jolly impatience, amused exasperation.

He waved us into chairs, saying, "Honest to Christ, I wish to hell Herm had the habit of writing things down. Nothing against him, you understand. Nobody ever had a better partner. But he carried around too much in his head alla time! It's driving me up the wall trying to find out who did what to who."

"I suppose," Meyer said, "you divided up all the responsibilities you have here."

"I've got the fat farm and the tennis club, and we'll have a riding stable going pretty soon. They're working on the stalls down there now." He swiveled his chair half around and pointed through the wide window to an old barn a hundred yards away. Two pickup trucks and a van were parked there, near a pile of fresh lumber. Off to the left a clutch of fatties trotted heavily down a long gentle slope. They were mostly women in their middle years, with a few men and a few adolescents, boys and girls. Despite the age differences, the fat at that distance looked the same, bouncing and flapping under the sweaty shorts and shirts. A lean woman was galloping along beside them, clapping her hands, running back and forth.

"We work the tract-house part together," he said. "I mean, we did. Herm handled the land sales. He was a wizard at that. We're all going to miss him. Of course, we both worked with the manager, Morse Slater. Morse keeps everything running smooth. If he wasn't around at this time, I'd be whipped. We lost a hell of a good girl right after we lost Herm. Some kind of legionnaire flu, they say. She wasn't here long, but Morse says she was the greatest. Everything from doing the billing to teaching tennis. Hell, it's a sound operation here. Everything will turn out roses. We've got a nice community coming along. We're keeping a lot of open space, and nothing tacky gets built. What was it you had going with Herm, gentlemen? Was it something to do with the commercial area?"

"Actually," Meyer said, "we're trying to find out who it was who flew in almost three weeks ago, maybe November twenty-eighth or -ninth, to talk to Mr. Ladwigg, and flew out the next morning."

"In a little blue airplane," Broffski said. His voice was no longer amiable, his face no longer jolly. "I am getting damn sick and tired of that fucking blue airplane. I am going to close that strip. Who needs it?"

He bounded up and went around us to his office door. "Morse! Get in here a minute."

Morse Slater came in, recognized me at once, and came over to me. I stood up, and he shook my hand and said, "I'm terribly sorry I had to miss the service, Mr. McGee. I thought until the last minute I would make it, but something came up."

I said, "Sure. Understood. Meyer, this is Morse Slater. I told you about him."

As they shook hands Broffski said, "What's going on? What service?"

"Gretel Howard," I told him.

There was a sudden look of comprehension. "McGee! Right. I heard about you from her. What has all this got to do with the fucking blue airplane?"

Meyer said politely, "Has someone else been interested in it?"

"We had the FAA out here. You tell them what it was about, Morse."

We all sat down and Morse said, "Apparently it was some sort of serious violation of the air safety rules, flying too close to a commercial liner, something like that. It was a Mr. Ryan from Washington, a field investigator, and they had traced the plane here. He was a very stubborn man. He couldn't seem to accept the idea that no one except Mr. Ladwigg knew where the airplane came from or who was flying it. He insisted on talking to some of the other employees, and he even had me take him over to the Ladwigg home and let him interrogate Mrs. Ladwigg."

"Catherine didn't know from nothing," Broffski said. "She never saw the guy. She said Herm put him up in the guest wing and talked business in there from the time he arrived until late at night. Herm told her not to bother about dinner, and when she checked the guest wing after the man had left, she found paper bags and cups from one of the fried chicken places down the Drive, so she thinks Herm went out and brought food back. The next morning early she heard Herm drive out in the Toyota. All Herm ever told her was that it was a big deal for a good-sized tract, and they were talking construction and deadlines. Damned imposition for him to go bothering Catherine."

Morse Slater said, "Ryan said to me that he wanted to find out if the aircraft had flown in from the islands with a load of coke or grass. He said he wanted to get that pilot out of the air. He just couldn't understand why we didn't have some record of the identification number on the plane. I showed him the strip, of course. A grassy strip, an old shed, a wind sock, and a padlocked gas pump. There's nobody there to check anything in or out."

"We let Ryan look through Herm's desk notes and appointment calendar," Stanley Broffski said. "He said he'd come back with a subpoena if we didn't. There wasn't a clue."

"When was Ryan here?" Meyer asked.

Slater stared at the ceiling for a moment. "Last Thursday, the thirteenth. He disrupted the day, most of it."

"Remember his whole name?" Meyer asked.

"Ryan, Howard C. In his forties. Pale, broad, soft. Very autocratic. An irritating fellow."

"I still don't understand why you two men are here," Broffski said. "Why should you give a shit who flew in and out in that airplane? What should it have to do with you?"

I reached into the deepest pocket in one of the old bags of tricks and came up with a useful inspiration. I leaned forward, adjusting my face to maximum leaden sincerity, and I secretly apologized to Gretel. "Mr. Broffski, I was able to be with Gretel for a little time every hour, while she was dying. Toward the end there, she came sort of half-awake, and she said, 'Blue airplane. Blue airplane.' I thought she was out of her head from the fever. If she wasn't, then she was trying to tell me something, I don't know what it was, and then when I heard from somebody at the funeral that a blue airplane had landed here the week before she died, I thought . . . well, it wouldn't be any harm in asking, because you were her friends."

"No harm! No harm at all!" Broffski said. "She was one terrific personality. She had star quality around here. Now I know why you're asking, but I still don't see what it has to do with anything. Herm knew who came in, and it seems as if whoever it was wanted to keep a real low profile."

"I wonder why," Morse Slater said, frowning.

"Who knows?" Broffski said. "Maybe some kind of deal he wasn't ready to tell us about. So if somebody is still interested, they'll contact us. If they do, I hope it's better than that Brussels deal of his."

"Brussels?" Meyer asked politely.

"Twenty acres, undeveloped, on the west side of the property," Slater said. "We're holding a ten percent deposit in an escrow account. The purchaser is something called the Morgen Group. Morgen with an 'e.' "

"Fascinating name," Meyer said.

"What's so fascinating about it?" Broffski asked.

"It's an obsolete land-measurement term which used to be used in Holland and in South Africa. A *morgen* is approximately two acres, and the translation, of course, is 'morning.' It derived from approximately how much land one man could plow with horses in a single morning."

Broffski stared at him. "You got a lot of stuff like that in your head? What line of work are you in?"

"I'm an economist. Semiretired."

"The address is a bank in Brussels. I tried to pick it up where Herm left off, and I made four phone calls to that bank. They deny any knowledge of the Morgen Group. All they would say is I should write to that name care of the bank, and if there was a Morgen Group, it would probably be delivered to them. I sent a cable, and the call-back on it said it was undeliverable. I wrote, and we're waiting."

Meyer nodded and said, "The Morgen Group is probably equivalent in law to what we call a blind trust here. And Brussels is quietly taking the place of Switzerland. Their secrecy is guaranteed by Belgian law. They have number accounts and investment services and they have no reverse interest, as the Swiss do. Thus, with a blind trust, there is a double layer of legal confidentiality. Impenetrable."

"Why so secret?" Broffski said. "Herm told me that a bunch of Belgians wanted to build their own hotel-club on the twenty acres, so the members could come here on vacation."

"Maybe it was going to be a front for something," Slater said.

Broffski looked across the desk at Slater, a look of annoyance and derision. "Sure. Right here in our back yard they are going to build a warehouse for the drug business. Or a studio to make porn movies."

"Sorry," Slater said. But he didn't look sorry.

Broffski sighed. "Well, there isn't anything I can do about it. The land sits there. Eleven months from now we can take the money out of escrow and put the land on the market again. Or develop it. Whatever." He stood up and reached across the desk. "Sorry we can't give you any more help." He shook hands, and we went out with Morse Slater.

"Can we look around the property?" Meyer asked.

"Certainly," he said, and gave us a brochure with a map of Bonnie Brae, showing the existing roads and the ones to come later. He pointed to the area on the map where the Belgians had planned to buy—and maybe still would. We thanked him and went out into the silver daylight, squinting against the high hard dazzle of the sky.

6

We walked across a field to the airstrip. We walked
through a healthy growth of sand spurs and stopped
and picked them off socks and pants cuffs when we
got to a cleared space. Meyer thumped the surface
of the landing strip with his heel.

"Probably some kind of soil cement," I said.
"You plow it up, mix the cement with the dirt,
grade it, water it, roll it down. Quick and easy."

We could hear the unrhythmic whacking of a lot
of hammers as workmen were framing a house a
hundred yards away.

Meyer said, "If Ladwigg was coming over here
to the strip from those houses there, cross-country,

he would have to pass that patch of bushes and palmetto over there."

We went over to look for tire tracks. They would
be about three weeks old. There was a faint pattern
in the heavy grass, a mark of rugged tread in dried
mud, and some grease stains on the tallest grass.

"So she stood here, I'd guess," Meyer said.

"Out in the early morning, looking for her pin,"
I said. "Yes. And so what?"

Meyer shrugged. "I don't *know* what. Every action we take, every thought we have, they are all
based upon some form of information. We know
more now than we did before. It is difficult, I think,
and erroneous, to try to decide in advance whether
additional facts will be useful."

"So if she stood here, and heard the motor and
stepped out in this direction, okay, the car would
pass close, and the passenger would be three feet
away, as she said. And we could backtrack the vehicle to old Herm's house. Incidentally, coming
around to the airstrip overland instead of on the
road doesn't mean much. The people who own
those four-wheel-drive brutes like to take them
bouncing through the fields and woods. It does
something for their glands. It could be preference
instead of secretiveness. On the other hand, he did
avoid meeting Mrs. Ladwigg, and the two men ate
in the guest wing. Anyway, Meyer, where the hell
are we *going* with all this?"

Roaring at Meyer seldom does any good. He

gave me the mild smile, the bland nod. "Let's see where we've been. On the thirteenth of December, two days before Toomey and Kline paid a visit to you, a Mr. Ryan visited Bonnie Brae. I do not think the Federal Aviation Administration gets into the business of tracking down small planes which endanger scheduled airline flights. I think that is the Civil Aeronautics Board's chore. And, whoever was looking into it, surely if there was danger of a collision, somebody would have picked up the identification numbers of the small airplane. They are required to carry the numbers in very large contrasting colors. Additionally, the customs people are monitoring all small planes in flight along this coast. And, finally, there seems to be a telltale monotony about the names of the three alleged officials—Howard C., Robert A., and Richard E. If any more turn up, we can expect William B. and Thomas D."

Meyer will never cease to astonish me. That heavy skull is loaded with microprocessors. Information is subject to constant analysis, synthesis, storage and retrieval. But when this makes him seem too intellectual, too somber, I have but to recall him at Bailey's, our neighborhood disco, cavorting like a dancing bear with three blond chiclets who adore him, and who listen to him when he sits like a hairy Buddha, declaiming instant legends and inventing instant folk-song lyrics. The dancing Meyer, pelt gleaming under the disco lights, little blue eyes shining, is the antidote to the data-pro-cessing machine under the skull bones.

We moved over into the semishade of a young live oak. The shadows had no edges under that white fluorescent sky.

He leaned against the tree. I sat on my heels and poked at the hard dirt with a piece of branch.

"It's too much!" he said irritably.

"How do you mean?"

"Pretend for one moment that Gretel never told us about Brother Titus. She might not have said anything, you know. Then where would we be? You would have accepted their story that they were looking into something that might be going on at Bonnie Brae. Let's hope they accepted your state-ment that Gretel had told you nothing. The Ryan person convinced them out at Bonnie Brae that he was what he said he was. Toomey, Kline, and Ryan were mopping up. There is no other answer. Lad-wigg and Gretel were both killed."

"No!"

"Yes, Travis. Both deaths were made to look routine. An accident and an illness. They would not make waves. It was somehow terribly important that no one be left alive who could talk about Brother Titus. The secrecy of the whole business in-dicates that there might be people who might pos-sibly recognize him. It was a remote chance, but one that X could not accept. Remember, I am using X to indicate an individual or an organization. Because of the emphasis on secrecy, I am assuming some link between Brother Titus and the twenty acres on which the Morgen Group made a down payment."

"But there wouldn't be any point in killing Gretel! What if she did recognize him? No matter *what* is going on, isn't that one hell of an overreaction to being recognized?"

"That's where I draw a blank, Travis. I have been trying to think of something big enough and bad enough and important enough for an organized group—and believe me, they *are* organized—to wipe out every possible trace of a visit from an official of an obscure religious sect. Eradication per se would not be difficult if one had the stomach for extreme measures. Float you out on the tide, and me also, to be totally safe. Eliminate Catherine Ladwigg, Stanley Broffski, Morse Slater, and anybody else Gretel worked with. Eradication of every trace without arousing suspicion is a lot trickier. It requires thought and organization and great care. If Gretel had not talked to you, it would have been successful. If you had been entirely truthful with Toomey and Kline, it would have been successful, because they would have dealt with you."

"Melodrama."

"I know. I know. But fit the facts together in any other way and you get more nonsense instead of less."

"So the Morgen Group was going to build some

kind of top-secret installation at Bonnie Brae. Or a heroin refinery. Or maybe Brother Titus was the fellow behind the grassy knoll in Dallas. Come on, Meyer. How many coincidences can we string together?"

I stood up and headed back across the field to the new asphalt road. I saw something glint in the grass, and bent down and pushed the grass aside and picked it up. I had seen her wear that pin several times when we had gone ashore from *The Busted Flush* during our long slow trip back around the peninsula. It was of Mexican silver, framing a three-dimensional Aztec face carved out of a mottled hard green stone. It was crudely made, and the clasp was not very secure.

How many coincidences can we string together? Sure. If, retracing her jogging route, she had found the pin before Ladwigg drove Titus back to his airplane—if she and her ex-husband had not traced her sister-in-law to that California encampment—if she had found a different job in Lauderdale . . .

Looking down at the primitive green face in the palm of my hand, I felt dizzy. The world was all tied together in some mysterious tangle of invisible web, single strands that reached impossible distances, glimpsed but rarely when the light caught them just right.

The biggest if of all. If she had never met me. Because I had brought her here.

If her mother had never met her father.

If her aunt had wheels.

If.

An empty path to walk. It leads toward superstition and paranoia, two whistle stops on the road to incurable depression. Once upon a time I took a random walk across a field. I went hither and yon, ambling along, looking at the sky and the trees, nibbling grass, kicking rocks. The first jeep to start across that field blew up. So did the people who went to get the people who'd been in the jeep. And I stood right there, sweaty and safe, trembling inside, while the experts dug over ninety mines out of that field, defused them, stacked them, and took them away. That's the way it goes sometimes. Philosophy 401, with Professor McGee. Life is a minefield. Think that over and write a paper on it, class.

I put the pin in my pocket. Talisman of some kind. Rub the tiny green face with the ball of the thumb. Like a worry stone, to relieve executive tensions. The times I remembered seeing it, she had worn it on the left side, where the slope of the breast began. She had bought it, she said, at a craft shop in San Francisco at Girardelli Square. I hadn't been there with her. All the places I hadn't been with her, I would never be with her. And at those unknown places, at unknown times, there would be less of me present. There can be few things worse than unconsciously saving things up to tell someone you will never see again.

"Coincidence," I told Meyer. "Maybe there was

somebody thinking about hustling her on her way, but they didn't have to. She got sick. And antibiotics wouldn't touch it. And she died."

"Maybe," he said. "Maybe it was that way."

My phone aboard the *Flush* rang at eight fifteen the next morning, and when I answered it I heard the click of someone hanging up. Fifteen minutes later it rang again, and when I answered it, a voice said, "Remember this number, McGee. Seven-nine-two, oh-seven-oh-one. Go to a pay phone as soon as you can and call this number. Seven-nine-two, oh-seven-oh-one."

He hung up. The voice was soft. There was no regional accent. I wrote the number down and finished my coffee while I thought about it. Then I locked up and walked to a pay phone.

The same voice answered. "This is McGee," I said.

"What was your mother's maiden name?"

"Devlin. Mary Catherine Devlin."

"Drive to Pier Sixty-six and park in the marina lot. Walk to the hotel and go in one of the lower-level entrances that face toward the marina, the one nearest the water. Turn right and walk slowly down the corridor toward the main part of the hotel."

"Why?"

After a pause he said, "Because you want to know why somebody died."

"Who the hell are you?"

"Can you remember what I told you to do?"

"Of course."

He hung up. I went to Meyer's stubby little cabin cruiser, the *John Maynard Keynes,* and roused him. He came out, blinking into the sunlight, carrying his coffee onto the fantail, looking grainy and whiskery. I repeated the two conversations as accurately as I could.

"Mother's maiden name. Standard security procedure. Not generally available."

"I know that. Somebody wants to tell me why Gretel died."

"You're going, of course."

"That's why I came over to tell you. So you'll be able to give somebody a lead if I don't show up back here. If somebody wants to take me out, forget the hotel. It will be the marina parking lot. Drop me there at long range, and untie the lines and take off."

"I'll come along."

"If you wouldn't mind. He didn't say to come alone. You could wait in the truck. Armed."

"But not very dangerous."

"What we will have are those stupid walkie-talkies, the little ones you bought as a gag. With fresh batteries. The mysterious strangers are probably in one of those rooms. I am assuming more than one. I can keep my unit in my pocket. Without my aerial up you should be able to read a signal from me based on Off-On. We can test them here."

With fresh batteries we found out that he would receive a definite alteration in the buzzing sound when my unit was turned on, even at a hundred yards. I could give him numbers. Short bursts for numbers from 1 to 9. A steady blast for a zero. Room 302 would be *dit-dit-dit daaaaah dit-dit*.

"In a building with a steel frame?" he asked.

"Listen harder. They'll take it away from me pretty quick, I imagine. I'll give you the room number soon as I can."

There are a lot of trees in that parking lot, and it has a considerable depth. I circled around the back of it, walking swiftly through the open areas. Then I circled back to an arched entrance, went in, turned right, walked slowly. The rooms were on my right. So they could have watched me through a window.

I kept my hand in my pocket, finger on the switch. A door opened behind me and I spun around. Room 121. Very easy. A sallow young man, tall, with a lot of nose and a lot of neck, motioned to me to come in. He wore pale-blue trunks, and he had a bath towel around his neck. His hair was still wet from his morning swim.

The familiar voice was right behind me, and I had neither heard him nor sensed him. "Hand out of the pocket. That's nice. Move right on in. Fine. You're doing fine."

With the voice still behind me and the room door

closed, the swimmer patted me down and took the little gadget out of my pocket. He read the label on it aloud. "Junior Space Cadet." He grinned and tossed it onto one of the double beds. "Clean," he said.

"Sit right down over there, in the straight chair by that countertop, Mr. McGee," the voice said. Large room. Two double beds. Pile carpeting. Small refrigerator. Recently redecorated. Between the half-open draperies I could see beach chairs and a table on the tiny ground-level terrace outside sliding doors, and I could look out toward the marina parking lot.

When I sat down I got my first look at the voice. Like Swimmer, he seemed to be in his late twenties. Mid-height, with the shoulder meat of one who works out with weights. Glossy dark hair, square jaw, neck as broad as the jaw. Metal-rimmed glasses with a slight amber tint. A pleasant smile.

"My name is McGee," I said.

"I think we'll try to get along without names."

He took the toy off the bed, inspected it, pulled the sectional aerial to full length, and went over and opened the sliding door. "Dr. Meyer? Everything is in order here. Why don't you come on in?"

When there was no answer, he tossed the unit to me. I pushed the little piano key and said, "No reason why you shouldn't, Meyer."

"Okay." The voice was tinny and remote. "Shall I bring your hat?"

John D. MacDonald

"No. Leave it in the car and lock up. Room One-two-one."

When Meyer arrived, Swimmer frisked him, declared him clean, and then winked at me and said, "I was looking for your hat."

"Was it all that obvious?" I asked.

"Don't worry about it," Weightlifter said. "It's good procedure. Simple and useful. Keep it. Because it doesn't work with us doesn't mean it isn't any good. But, Dr. Meyer, I'm curious."

"Just Meyer, please."

"Fine. What if he'd asked you to bring his hat?"

"There are several ways he could have asked me to bring it. Each one is an option. If he felt the two of us could handle things, I would have been ready when I came through the door, and so would he."

"Nice. Very nice," Swimmer said.

"You seem to know a hell of a lot," I said.

Weightlifter shrugged and sat on the edge of a bed, and motioned Meyer over to a wing chair by the sliding doors. "Not as much as we tried to find out. I'll give you credit. You have some very solid friends around that marina, McGee. We didn't have much time to work on it. We put a lot of people on it. We pulled your military record. We put some tourists into that Bahia Mar Marina. We had somebody at Timber Bay. We sent somebody to Petaluma. We know—or at least we feel able to assume—that you are not wanted anywhere, that

90

your identity is correct, that you are not into the coke or grass trade, and that you are not political."

"Who is we?" Meyer asked.

"We won't go into that. Just as I told Mr. McGee, we won't go into names either. And we won't show identification. And if you check the register later, it won't do you a bit of good. And, I'll be frank with you, the names and the connections wouldn't mean much to you. We are going to ask questions. Lots of them. This might take a long time. But we start with evidence of good faith."

Swimmer went to the closet and came back with a nine-by-twelve manila envelope and handed it to Weightlifter.

"Before I show you these," Weightlifter said, "I must explain how we happened to luck out. Dr. Tower reported the symptoms to the Center for Disease Control in Atlanta. They have had standing orders for over a year to report any case which has those same symptoms to a certain branch of the Federal Government. An expert in forensic medicine flew down to Atlanta from New York, starting about an hour after word came to Washington. When it became obvious to Dr. Tower that Mrs. Howard was going to die, he phoned Atlanta. The expert came down here in time to participate in the autopsy. He found what we had instructed him to look for. Take a look at these prints."

I had been watching him covertly. He was left-handed. He wore a sport shirt that hung outside his trousers, and once when he moved I had identified the bulge on his right side, halfway between the belly button and the point of the hip bone.

He handed me the print, and when he turned to take the other one over to Meyer, I let mine slip to the floor, moved quickly behind him, locked his left arm, and reached around and under with the right hand and yanked the belly holster out, gun, belt clip, and all, and then slammed him into Swimmer, who was heading for the closet. They went into a lamp table and snapped a couple of slender legs as they brought it down.

By then I had the short-barreled revolver properly in hand, and Meyer was standing beside me.

"Slow and easy," I said, and they did indeed move slowly as they separated themselves from each other and from the pieces of lamp and table. There was nothing pleasant about their faces, but nothing ugly either. No sign of strain or worry. A watchful competence, like a very good boxer waiting for the opening.

I have to go on instinct. Sometimes it has betrayed me. Never fatally, fortunately. Most of the time it works for me.

I said, "We'll play it your way, gentlemen. I didn't want you to go away with the impression we're a pair of clowns. It is a matter of pride with me. Let's say our relationship has reached a new level. First names would help."

I tossed the gun onto the nearest bed and extended my hand to Weightlifter. As he took it and I pulled him to his feet, he said, "Max. He's Jake."

Jake got up and cocked his head as he stared at me. "Maybe if I hadn't read off the name of that walkie-talkie?"

"Maybe. I don't know."

Max slid the revolver into the holster after checking it over, and clipped the holster to his pants and smoothed the sport shirt down over the bulge. He looked thoughtful. "McGee, you may be half again as big as I expected, and you are certainly twice as quick as anybody your size I've ever seen, but it was still a hell of a risk. It was a stupid risk. You miss the gun and maybe I kill you as I am falling. From instinct. From training. From too long doing what I do."

"He wanted to make an impression on you," Meyer said.

Jake said, "There are some folks we work with and work for who would never let us forget how we got taken."

"And never understand it," Max said.

"But they weren't here to watch," I said.

I saw the tension going out of him, little by little. Jake had a bad bruise on his shin. It was swelling and turning blue. I had torn a fingernail snatching the revolver.

Finally Max grinned at me and said, "Now I understand a little bit more about some of the things I found out about you. Now they make more sense. But it was still stupid."

Meyer made an odd sound. He looked up from the print he was holding. He looked questioningly at Max and said, "Markov?"

"Yes. And you better tell me how you know about that!"

7

Meyer looked at Max, his expression puzzled. "But why wouldn't I know about it? It had a lot of publicity."

"But how would you make the connection from these photographs?"

Still puzzled, Meyer said, "The details made an impression on me." He looked toward the ceiling, frowned, closed his eyes, and said, "A sphere of platinum and iridium—I forget the percentages of each in the alloy. One fifteenth of an inch in diameter, with two tiny holes drilled into it at right angles to each other, with traces of an unknown substance in the holes."

"But you glanced at these photos and made the connection."

Meyer straightened and glared at him. "If you are pretending to be professional, *act* like a professional. If I had any trace of guilty knowledge, would I have revealed it? The people who *do* have guilty knowledge are certainly too professional to reveal it."

I interrupted, saying, "Let me explain something. Meyer has a fantastic memory. I don't know what the hell either of you are talking about. What I've got here is a picture of what looks like a lumpy silver bowling ball with the holes drilled badly."

"The scale, Travis," Meyer said. "Look at the scale."

Yes, it was very small. Maybe not quite as small as the head of a pin, but almost.

"That item," said Max, "is a twin to the one removed from the right thigh of a Bulgarian defector in London named Georgi Markov after he died—with the symptoms of high fever, sharp drop in blood pressure, and renal failure. That was quite some time ago."

"Somebody jabbed him with an umbrella," Meyer said.

"Yes. That one. This is a photograph of an identical object removed from the right side of the back of the neck of Mrs. Howard. The traces of the poison found inside those holes are being analyzed. They did not get a complete analysis of the poison in the Markov case, or in the Kostov attempt which happened a month before Markov was killed. The pellet hit Kostov in the back in a Paris subway. We can assume a better delivery system was devised to take care of Markov. Kostov recovered."

I sat heavily and stared at the picture of the dull silver ball. Somebody had stuck that thing into the back of the neck of my woman and killed her. I had been trying not to accept the fact that such a thing could happen, and had happened.

"I'm burning up. I feel terrible, Trav. Terrible."

Her face had become gaunt so quickly. Fever had eaten her up, eaten the quickness and happiness, eaten the brightness.

The reason for doing that to her seemed beyond any comprehension. But somebody did it. And from this moment on, the only satisfying purpose in life would be to find out exactly, precisely, specifically who.

I came back from a long way off and heard the last part of Meyer's question. "—many more since the Markov case?"

"Classified information."

"Who *does* such a thing?" I demanded.

Jake took the answer to that one. "We could say that we have reason to believe the poison itself, a complex chemical structure, was developed by Kamera, a section of Department V of the KGB. We have reason to believe they have been working for many years on poisons which, after injection, break down into substances normally found in the human body. They killed Vladimir Tkachenko back in 1967 in London when, we think, he tried to defect. Method of delivery unknown. Poison unknown."

"It's like you're speaking a foreign language. This is Fort Lauderdamndale. This is the palm-tree Christmas coming, with Sanny Claus in shorts, and the tourists swarming. What has all this Russian stuff got to do with Gretel and me?"

Max said, "It has something to do with everyone who lives on the planet, in one way or another."

"Philosophy I don't need," I said.

"Okay. Markov, most probably, was killed by an agent from the Soviet bloc. He was making the big man in Bulgaria, Todor Zhivkov, very unhappy by his broadcasts over Radio Free Europe. We can guess that Zhivkov asked for help to get him silenced. But when it comes to the assassination of a young woman in Florida, we can't make the same kind of reasonable assumption. Put it this way. Russia and the United States are each supportive of various groups and movements all over the world. Arms and ammunition move toward areas of tension. There is no way to exert final control over the use of a weapon. The two major powers try to supply those whose goals are closest to their own, and then they hope for the best. This is a very advanced and exotic assassination device. We can assume the KGB would be cautious about supplying it to anyone over here. We could have missed it easily. When they took a scrap of tissue for biopsy while Mrs. Howard was still alive, they could have gotten that platinum bead along with it, missed it when they sliced a section for the microscope, and thrown it out without ever knowing. So the intent was to simulate a natural death. That leads us to the point. Why could she not be permitted to live? Why did it have to look like a natural death?"

I looked at each of them in turn. "And that's it? You don't know who did it?"

Max shook his head. "We have no idea. We can't find a starting point, except with you two."

Meyer asked, "What kind of people would it be rational for them to supply over here with a thing like that?"

Max shrugged. "A mole, maybe. Somebody who was put in place a long time ago. Any agitator of any consequence. Weathermen, Symbionese, anybody trying to alter the political equilibrium by violent means. But that doesn't make it sound rational. It doesn't seem like a useful target. One would expect it should be a visiting shah, a premier, or a red-hot research physicist. Let's get to it. Mr. McGee, do you have any reason to believe that Gretel Howard was connected in any way with any political action group?"

I looked down at my fists as I sought the right way to say it. "We had a lot of intense time alone with each other. A couple of months aboard my houseboat. We talked a lot. We opened up to each other all the way. We tracked each other from childhood right on up to the moment. She was as apolitical as I am. We both lived in the world, and didn't get too red-hot about who was running it. Maybe that's wrong in your eyes. But it is the way she was and the way I am."

"And she could not have been conning you?"

"Absolutely no way."

"When and how did she get the alleged insect sting?"

"No idea. She was telling me over the phone everything that had gone wrong with her day. No, sorry. She didn't tell me about the insect bite until I saw her in the hospital. She broke a mug I had given her when she was having breakfast, and then she learned her boss had fallen off his bike and died, and then a bug bit her, and then she had fainted and fallen and broken a lamp in the Ladwigg house. From the sequence I'd say she got bitten, or shot, between eight and ten o'clock that morning. How was it done?"

Jake shook his long sandy head. "The thing is so damn small, delivery systems are difficult. It has so little mass it makes a poor projectile. Like a man trying to hurl a single grain of rice. One of the groups . . . I mean to say, we've experimented with silver beads which closely approximate the size and weight of one of the deadly ones. The propulsion force can be compressed air, a spring mechanism, or a small charge of propellant. Compressed air seems to provide the most convenient, quiet, and compact unit. But for it to penetrate the skin, the maximum effective range is about ten inches. Beyond that, the lack of mass reduces velocity and penetrating power drastically. So someone had to put the weapon within a few inches of her neck. It could have looked like a book, a camera, a walking stick, a tobacco pipe, a purse—almost any small unremarkable portable object. The best time and place would be out of doors, in a crowd."

"Like a crowd around Ladwigg after he fell?" I said.

"Yes, like that," Max said. "Here's the scenario. Ladwigg's early morning bike ride had been cased. Somebody picked the right spot, out of sight of any of the houses, where they could step out and chunk a rock into the front of his face as he came along at twenty miles an hour on his ten-speed. When the body was discovered, the sirens arriving brought people out of the houses widely scattered around there. And the people from the offices. It's a new community. For the most part, the people are strangers to each other. An unfamiliar person would be assumed to be a new homeowner. When they got Markov, they poked him in the back of the leg with an umbrella tip. Mrs. Howard got it in the back of the neck, so, as I said, the weapon could have looked like any innocuous familiar object. And the crowd watching them load Ladwigg's body provided enough diversion. After we learned what had killed the woman and went back in time and took a closer look at the way Ladwigg died, it became obvious they were part of the same assignment for somebody."

"If you know that," I said, "then you've probably done a lot more homework. Why don't you tell us what you know, so we won't be repeating stuff?"

"It's better this way. It's a check on our own information."

"And on us."

"Why not? Memories aren't flawless. Don't have such a low boiling point. Your honor isn't at stake any more," Max said.

"So ask me something."

Meyer interrupted. "Gentlemen!" he said. "Let's all be friends. I think that what I will do at this point is relate the details of a visit by two men to Mr. McGee last Saturday, a visit by one man to Bonnie Brae on Thursday, the thirteenth, some phone calls I made yesterday morning, and a visit to Bonnie Brae which we made yesterday afternoon. But before I get into that narrative, I will first tell you what Gretel Howard told the two of us on the evening of Friday, December seventh. Knowing your area of interest and suspecting the extent of your training, I shall tell this in what may seem like infinite detail, adding my suspicions, inferences, and conjectures as I proceed. Will that be useful?"

"Very."

"Before I begin, let me say that I am taking you two on faith. I am assuming your hats are white. Left to my own devices, I would not be so revelatory. But when my friend Travis threw the revolver onto the bed, he was exercising his right to have a hunch, and because I have seen how his hunches usually work, I am following it."

I moved over to a more comfortable chair. Jake taped the extraordinary performance. Meyer remembered so much more than I did, I wondered if my brain was slowly turning to mush. He spoke in sentences, in paragraphs, in chapters. Max scribbled a note to himself from time to time. Whenever I thought Meyer was going to leave something out, he came around to it in the next few minutes. When he was through he was slightly hoarse, and we took a break and ordered up a late room-service lunch. Jake intercepted the cart at the door, signed, and wheeled it in.

During lunch there were some obligatory comments about the weather, the price of hotel rooms, the Miami Dolphins' season, and how much vitamin C you take to ward off the common cold.

After the cart was wheeled out again by Jake and the door closed, Max got up and paced, frowning, chunking his fist into his palm from time to time.

He went back to the desk and looked at his notes. "Give me her description of this Brother Titus again, please. As close to her words as you can make it."

"I can make it exact," Meyer said.

"How the hell can you do that?"

"Give me a couple of minutes," Meyer said. He closed his eyes and began to breathe slowly and deeply. His eyelids fluttered. His mouth sagged partly open. I had seen him do it before. It was a form of autohypnosis, and he was projecting himself back to the evening of the seventh.

He lifted his head and opened his eyes. Jake inserted a fresh cassette and punched the tape on again. Meyer spoke in his own voice and diction. "Big, but not fat. Big-boned. About forty, maybe a little less. Kind of a round face, with all of his features sort of small and centered in the middle of all that face." It made the backs of my hands tingle and the back of my neck crawl. It was Gretel's word choice, phrasing, cadence, pauses. It was Gretel, speaking again through Meyer, telling us whom to look for.

"Wispy blond hair cut quite short. No visible eyebrows or eyelashes. Lots and lots of pits and craters in his cheeks, from terrible acne when he was young. Little mouth, little pale eyes, girlish little nose. He was wearing a khaki jacket over a white turtleneck. He was holding onto the side of the passenger door because of the rough ride. His hands are very big and . . . well, brutal-looking."

He stopped and gave himself a little shake, and all three of them looked questioningly at me.

"Absolutely exact," I said. "Just as I remember it. I mean, better than I remember it." I was too boisterous, too jovial, too loud, the way you get when you want to disavow being moved by something. I caught Meyer's look of concern. I envied him his ability to regress himself to the actual scene, to be with her in that way. I had no way to be with her. Memory has a will of its own. When I forced it, she would blur out. It had to come to me in sudden takes, little snippets from the cutting-room floor of the mind. They came smoking in, stunning me.

The tape was stopped. Jake had put the cassettes in a row, in order. He began numbering them, dating them.

Max looked at his notes. "When there is a near collision in the air, NASA is the investigating agency. They recommend to the FAA the action to be taken. So do the controllers and airport managers. We'll recheck the three of them—Toomey, Kline, and Ryan, but will come up probably with just what you have, Meyer."

Meyer nodded and said, "I keep thinking, Max, wondering what those three *do* represent. Travis caught that faint continental flavor. But he says the speech was colloquial American."

"Buffalo, St. Louis, or Santa Barbara," I said, "or anyplace in between. Middle height, middle age, no distinguishing features. Office fellows. Flabby and pale. Both with glasses. Invisible men. Clothes off the rack, not cheap and not expensive. Hell, if you walked through any downtown past the banks on a Tuesday noon, you'd see them walking together to lunch. If you lined up ten of them, I'd have a sorry job trying to pick out my two."

"You're describing the average, upper-echelon, middle-European, or Eastern European agent. They don't see enough daylight. They spend a lot of time on the files. They eat too much starch. And the KGB has the best language schools in the world. Crash courses, and they turn out people who can speak the language of the assigned country like a native. Of course, those guys are motivated. If they don't work hard enough learning the language, they end up in Magnitogorsk or some damn place, processing internal travel permits. They're good. Just not very flexible. They're not good at jettisoning one plan in mid-flight and inventing a second one that might work."

"But how could they fit into all this?" Meyer asked.

Max grinned at him. "You want another scenario? The way I read it, somebody goofed badly on something very important. So they sent Igor and Vashily here on a tidy-up mission. Plug the holes. Find out who knows what, report back, and await orders."

"Their presence would imply some importance to this."

Jake laughed, and snapped one of the eight-by-ten glossies with a fingernail. "You bet your ass there's something important going on. The presence of this little sphere proves that. We'll go through the Church of the Apocrypha to locate this Brother Titus and find out if he is coincidence or part of it somehow. I don't have much hope of unwinding anything in Brussels. We've bounced off that wall before. It's very tight over there."

Max stood up and said, "We're very grateful for your cooperation, gentlemen."

"Will you contact us again?" I asked.

"Doubtful."

"How would we get in touch with you?"

"Why should you?" There was some amusement in his steady gaze.

I said, "Who knows? Something else happens that fits in with this, who do we tell?"

Jake said to Max, "If we don't know what's going on, we don't know if they are involved more than they think they are. An identity mixup. Or something observed they shouldn't have seen."

After a moment of thought, Max nodded and wrote a number down and tore it out of his pad. "Memorize this number. Use a phone you can control for a couple of hours. It may take that long for a call-back. Here is what you say. That line will always answer, day and night. The person will say hello. You say, 'Was somebody at this number trying to reach Travis McGee?' They'll say they don't know, but they can check around and find out. Then you say, 'If anyone was, I can be reached at such and such a number.' Then wait. Clear?"

"Perfectly," I said.

Max stood a little taller and said, "You shouldn't have gone out to see Broffski and Slater. The cover story was halfway okay, but frail. What you shouldn't do, either of you or both of you, is push at this thing any more, from any direction. We've satisfied ourselves you can both keep your mouth shut about what you learned here. Finding out the kind of security clearance you had once upon a time, Meyer, helped in that decision. So lay low. Keep down. Keep quiet. In return for that, I promise I'll find some way to let you know when we've tidied up. No, don't leave just yet. I have to make a call."

He made it from a phone in a dispatch case. He grunted and listened, grunted and listened, then said thanks and hung up and slapped the case shut. "No sign of your being followed here. There's no directional bug on your pickup truck, and your home phones on those two boats are not tapped."

"She died a week ago today," I said. "She didn't want to die. She was pushed over the edge. She was pushed off the earth. And you want me to keep down and keep quiet."

Max looked at me with a pitying expression. "If

you wanted to thrash around, what could you do? Where could you start? Suppose you knew for sure that the DGI did it."

"What's the DGI?"

"The Cuban secret service. It has been directed and controlled by the KGB for nine years at least. What next? Who do you ask? Who do you go see? And who would know anything anyway? Is whoever killed her still alive? Maybe not. Intelligence operations are compartmentalized. There is only one contact between cells, and few people in any cell. I don't care what you do. Just don't go to the police to complain about an unsolved murder, and don't write your congressman about internal security."

"We can leave now?" Meyer asked.

Max nodded. Jake took a look at the corridor. We left. The day was the same kind of day. But the world was a different kind of world.

8

We were back aboard *The Busted Flush* by four o'clock. My brain seemed to be droning along in neutral. I could not kick it into gear.

Meyer selected a beer. I roamed back and forth with a beaker of Boodles on ice. "I don't want it to be depersonalized," I said. "I want it to be a single person with a single motive. I don't want it to be organizational, a committee decision. You can't get your hands around the throat of a committee. You can't beat the face of an organization against a brick wall."

"Listen to me, Travis. Stop pacing and listen. If she was killed because she discovered something, by pure accident, she should not have known, then it is accidental death. The world is full of secret plans and understandings. A sniper in Lebanon misses and the slug smashes the head of a child a half mile farther away. What can the child's father do? Who does he see? Where does he file his complaint?"

"Somebody aimed at her, Meyer, and didn't miss."

"And your chance of ever finding that somebody is exactly zero."

"Then I'll find who gave the orders."

"Again zero."

"How can you possibly know that?"

"Travis, please sit down. I can't talk to you when you keep walking around behind me. There. That's better. And if you can listen a little, it will be better yet. I live in two worlds, yours and the real world."

"Come on!"

"Just listen. In your world the evil is small scale. It is one on one. It is creature preying on creature. All right, so it can be terrifying. I am not trying to say it is like games in a sandbox under the apple tree. A person can get killed doing what you do, and I think it is a worthwhile way for you to live. In these past few years it has made you a bit morose, but that is only because any kind of repetition leads to a certain staleness of the soul. Too many beds, and too much dying. Greed and love begin to wear the same masks. Gretel gave me high hopes for you. You were emerging from the dolor of repetition. Now you look as if you had been hit on the head with a mallet. In your world, your heart is broken. I want to reach you before you start any kind of move that will break your heart on a larger scale than you can now conceive of. All right?"

"Keep talking."

"When I attend conferences on international monetary affairs, when I go give my little speeches, or go earn a little fee for consultation, I hear of many things. They alarm me. I cannot tell you how much they alarm me. In Iran a little band of schoolteachers dribble gasoline around the circumference of a movie house and light it, incinerating four hundred and thirty people, most of them children. In Guyana nine hundred Americans kill themselves, for reasons as yet unexplained. There are over four billion people in the world, and each day more and more of them are dying in bloody and sickening ways. The pot is beginning to simmer. The little bubbles appear around the edges. Intrigue, interconnected, is multiplying geometrically, helped along by the computer society. Orbiting eyes in the sky scan us all. Poisons abound. The sick birds fall out of the air. Signs and portents, Travis. And here we are in happyland, in a resort town, with the bright sunshine, bright boats, humid young ladies. This is all stage setting. Carnival. Scenario. The real world is out there in a slow dreadful process of change. There is a final agony of millions out there, and one and a quarter million new souls arriving every week. We try to think about it less than we used to. None of it makes any sense, really. But then whatever it is that is out there, it moves into this world in the shape of a tiny sphere of platinum and iridium and deadly poison. Now we have to think about it, but it cannot be personalized. It is all a *thing*, a great plated toadlizard thing with a rotten breath, squatting back inside the mouth of the cave, infinitely patient."

"So keep on having fun?"

"That's not very responsive."

"Sorry."

"Being an adult means accepting those situations where no action is possible."

"Except joining the Church of the Apocrypha."

"Have you lost your mind?"

"Brother Titus will forgive my sins."

"It's an idiotic idea."

"I have to go out to California anyway, with . . . the ashes."

"When are we leaving?"

I smiled at him and shook my head. "Not this time, Meyer. Part of this trip is trying to get away from myself somehow. I have no delight in what and who I am. Not any more. Not here."

Meyer sat and looked at me for a long moment, the small bright blue eyes intent, the face impassive. "You take yourself wherever you go, Travis."

"A popular truism."

He finished the beer and put it aside. "I'll go get the urn."

"You don't have to bother right now. I can come and get it when I'm ready to leave."

"I might not be there. I'll get it now."

He was back in ten minutes with a cardboard carton, a vise-grip wrench he had borrowed a year ago, and fifteen dollars he claimed he owed me and insisted I take.

And then he was gone. It had not occurred to me that I would hurt Meyer, but there seemed to be no point in going over and apologizing to him. Through me, he had acquired a taste for the salvage business. Now there was nothing left to save but myself. And he couldn't help me there.

I fixed myself another heavy drink and, carrying it along, I went through all the interior spaces of *The Busted Flush*. I remembered all the lovely women. I looked at the huge shower stall, the sybaritic tub, the great broad bed in the master stateroom. I looked at the speakers and turntables, the tape decks and tape racks. Everything had a sweet, sad look. Like a playpen with scattered toys after the child has died.

When the drink was gone, I went down to my hidey-hole in the forward hull and removed all my reserve and took it up to the lounge. Ninety-three hundred-dollar bills. Life savings. Wisely invested, it might bring me almost eighty dollars a month. I sat and planned what I would wear and what I would carry, and mentally distributed my fortune in inconspicuous places.

Then I looked directly at the cardboard carton for the first time. Firmly taped and tied. Ten inches square, twelve inches tall. All the remains of the physical Gretel. It hefted at about the weight of a sizable cantaloupe.

I sat at the little pull-down writing desk again, and I wrote a letter to Meyer:

> I will take this up to the office and give it to Linda and tell her to hold it a few days and then give it to you. By then I will have added the keys to this boat, and to the *Muñequita* and to the car. I will have emptied out the perishables and turned off the compressors and arranged for disconnect on the phone. I am enclosing five hundred in cash—I better make that eight hundred—to take care of expenses around here. I will have put the phone on temporary disconnect and arranged for my mail to come to you. Today is December 18th. If I am going to be able to make it back here, I will get word to you somehow on or before June 18th. If you don't hear by then, everything here belongs to you. Frank Payne has a will on file to that effect, witnessed and all. I don't really know what is mak-

ing me act the way I am acting. You would know more about that than I, probably. I have this very strong feeling that I am never coming back here, that this part of my life is ending, or that all of my life is ending. I have been bad company a lot of the time the past few years, going sour somehow. Gretel was the cure for that. I came back to life, but not for long. And this is what the stock market guys call a lower low. I just feel futile and ridiculous. You are the best friend I have ever had. Take care of yourself. Make a point of it. If I don't come back, what you should do is move aboard the *Flush,* peddle your crock boat and the *Muñequita* and the Rolls, and throw a party they will never never forget around here.

I put it in a heavy brown envelope and left it unsealed. It was dark. I took a walk around my weather decks. The night smelled like diesel fuel. A nearby drunk was singing "Jingle Bells," never getting past the sleigh, starting again and again and again. The boulevard hummed and rustled with cars, and there was no sound at all from the sea. A woman laughed, a jet went over, and I went back inside. Somebody working his way into his slip made a small wake, and the *Flush* shifted, sighed, and settled back into stillness.

On the following Saturday morning I found the same man at the Petaluma cemetery, the one Gretel and I had dealt with when we had flown out with John Tuckerman's ashes. He was cultivating and reseeding two parallel curving scars in the soft green turf. He was a broad muscular old man with a bald head and thick black eyebrows. He wore sneakers and crisp khakis. He dropped the tool, dusted his hands, and tilted his head to one side as he looked up at me.

"Weren't you here way last spring? With the Tuckerman girl?"

"With Gretel Howard. Her married name."

"What you got there?"

"Well . . . she died. Gretel died. This is her ashes."

He mopped his face and turned slightly away and looked upward into a tree. He sighed. "Sorry to hear it. Even if it was a sad time for her, bringing her brother's ashes here, it wasn't hard to see you and she were real close, real happy with each other."

"Yes, we were."

"Too bad. Nice size on that girl. Great smile. What did she die from? Automobile? That is what takes most of the young ones."

"Some kind of flu with a high fever and kidney failure."

"I tell people it's the bugs striking back. Those laboratories go after the bugs with powerful new poisons and it stands to reason that the ones that live through it, they get twice as tough and nasty as they ever were before. Of course, John and Gretel's folks, they died premature, but it wasn't sickness. I suppose you want her in the family plot. Dumb-ass question. You wouldn't be here if you didn't."

"Can we go right ahead with it?"

"Don't you remember how it was before? There's got to be the permit, and they've got to have vital statistics for the records, and there's the fee."

"The office is closed."

"I know. They used to stay open Saturday morning, but not lately."

"I've got a copy of the death certificate here, and I've got her birth certificate, marriage certificate, and final decree of divorce. Here, you can have them."

He took them and then tried to give them back to me, saying, "I don't have anything to do with the office part."

"And if the permit hasn't gone up since last time, here's the fifty dollars."

He hesitated and finally took it. "I guess we could do it now and I could give them this stuff Monday. But don't you want any words said? She said the words for her brother."

"As I will for her."

The Tuckerman plot was in that part of the cemetery where the stones were flush with the ground—which, as he had mentioned when I had seen him before, made mowing a lot easier. While he went to get the post-hole digger from his shed, I opened the carton. The urn was shinier than I had expected it to be, and more ornate. It looked like a large gold goblet with a lid.

She had owned a small worn book of the collected poems of Emily Dickinson. She had read two of them over her brother's grave. She had marked the ones she liked best. There were three short ones I wanted to read.

I could just make out the place where the old man had dug the hole before, for John Tuckerman's urn. He chose a new spot and asked me if it was all right. I approved of it and asked him if I could dig.

"Leave the dirt close and neat," he said.

He watched me as I chunked the tool down, lifting the bite of earth in the blades, setting it aside each time, close and neat. Once it was down over a foot, it began to get me in the small of the back. It is an awkward posture, an awkward way to lift.

When it was deep enough, he stopped me. I lifted the urn out of the box and, kneeling, lowered it to the bottom of the hole. I stood up then and read the first two poems, the longer ones. My voice had a harsh and meaningless sound in the stillness, like somebody sawing a board. I said the words I saw on the page without comprehending their meaning. Then I read the one she had read to her dead brother, called "Parting."

"My life closed twice before its close—
It yet remains to see
If Immortality unveil
A third event to me

"So huge, so hopeless to conceive
As these that twice befell.
Parting is all we know of heaven,
And all we need of hell."

I bent and dropped the faded blue book down the hole, and then, kneeling, using both hands, I cupped up the dirt and filled the hole and tamped it down, replaced the circle of turf I had cut with the digger, and with the edge of my hand brushed away the loose dirt into the grass roots.

"No marker for her either?" he asked.

"I don't think so. Neither of them had children to come and look for the place." The oblong of marble, level with the earth, reading TUCKERMAN, was enough.

"Those words were like the ones she read that time. Is that some kind of one of these new religions?"

"Sort of."

"I thought so. There's a lot of them these days. I guess having one is better than having none, but it makes you wonder." He looked down toward the office and the road. "Where'd you park?"

"I walked out from the bus station."

"Where are you going? Back to Florida?"

"I haven't decided."

"This town isn't as bad as some. If you need work, maybe I can think of somebody you could go ask. You look sort of down on your luck, mister."

"Thanks. If I come back this way, I'll look you up."

When I looked back from the road he was still watching me. I waved. He waved and turned away, back to his work fixing the scars where somebody had torn up the turf doing funny stunts in an automobile. I dug my duffel bag out of the bushes where I had hidden it and shouldered it with the wide strap over my left shoulder, the bag bumping against my right hip. My poncho was strapped to the duffel bag. I wore work shoes, dark-green twill trousers, a faded old khaki shirt, a brown felt hat, a gray cardigan sweater. I had sandy stubble on my jaws and neck. Before leaving Florida, I'd had my hair clipped down to a Marine basic cut, which could have been a prison cut. I carried in my shirt pocket, for the right occasion, a pair of glasses with gold-colored rims, hardly any correction in the lenses, and one bow fixed with black electrician's tape. I wanted to attract a second look from the av-

erage cop, but without stirring enough curiosity for
him to want to check me out. But if he did check
me out, I had some credentials. I had an expired
Florida driver's license with my picture on it, and I
had a fragile tattered copy of army discharge papers, and a social security card sandwiched in plastic. They were wrapped in a plastic pouch and were
in the compartment in the end of the duffel bag.
They all said I was Thomas J. McGraw, address
General Delivery, Osprey, Florida, occupation
commercial fisherman.

"Well, officer, it was like this. My old lady died
and I sold off our stuff and the trailer, and I
thought I'd come out here and poke around and see
if I could locate our daughter Kathy. She took off
six years ago when she was fourteen, and we heard
from her two years ago, some postcards from San
Francisco, and Petaluma and Ukiah. She said she
was joining up with some kind of church. Me, I
come here by Greyhound bus."

As I walked, I wrote my autobiography, and the
story of my marriage, and my wife's death. I made
Peg and Kathy into real people. I made Tom
McGraw into a real person. As I walked, I went
over and over the imaginary events of my life until
I could see them. I outlined my own personality. I
was not too quick of wit, and I tended to lose jobs
through getting drunk and not showing up. When I
worked, I was a hard worker. I was a man of great
pride. I did not suffer unkind remarks about my

character or my station in life. I was a womanizer when I was in my cups. Peg had been a staunch churchwoman. I went with her a couple times a year. I shared most of my political opinions with Archie Bunker. As I walked, I talked to imaginary people, talked as Tom McGraw would talk to them. He was servile when he talked to people in power. He was affable as a dog with his peers. He was nasty to those he considered beneath him. I worked my way into the role.

Long, long ago, I had known an actress. Susan was twenty-four. I was sixteen. She was working in summer theater. I was working in the country hotel where she was staying. She was a lanky lady who cussed, wore pants, and smoked thin little cigars. I found her monstrously exciting. I was worried about myself that year. There had been an episode with a loud chubby girl who, true to locker-room gossip, was willing to put out. But she was so loud that I was less than able. I could almost but not quite count it as the first time. I could lie to others but not to myself, and I had the dread fear Lolly would tell everybody. I was worried about myself.

Though I was a head taller than the actress, she didn't want to be seen with me around town. I would walk out into the country, and she would come along in her borrowed car and we would go up into the hills and park and go walking together. In August, after we had gotten into the habit of making a bed from a blanket and spruce bows, in hidden places, while we were resting from each other, I told her about Lolly and about my fears. She laughed her deep harsh startling laugh and told me that I had less to worry about than anybody she had ever known. It was very comforting.

It was repertory theater, and she had to refresh her memory in a lot of roles. It startled me the way she could turn herself into an entirely different person. We would sit in the shade and I would give her her cues from the playscript, and then we would walk and she would become the character in the play. I had to ask her questions, any questions, and she would respond as that person would have responded. She explained that it was the best way to do it. One had to invent a past that fitted, and memories that fitted. She explained that once you were totally inside a false identity, secure in it, you could handle the unexpected on stage in a way consistent with the character.

And I had used that afterward, many times, and now I was using it again. Susan taught me a lot. Once she got me past the initial shyness, she showed me and told me all the ways I could increase her pleasure while delaying mine. It gave me a wonderful feeling of domination and control to be able to turn that strong, tense, mature female person into gasping, grasping, shuddering incoherence. I was in love with her, of course. I could not stand the thought of the summer ending. I told her I loved her, and I was going to come to New York to be close to her.

I will always remember the way she cupped both hands on my face and looked deeply into my eyes. "Travis, you are a very very sweet boy, and you are going to become one hell of a man. But if I ever find you outside my apartment door, I am going to have the doorman throw you out on your ass. We can end it right now or next week, whichever you choose. But end it we will, boyo, with no loose ends. No letters, no phone calls, no visits. Ever."

And that's how it was.

So now I walked my way deeper into my Tom McGraw role. Trucks whuffed by, with the trailing turbulence tugging at my clothes. Divided highway. Route 101. Looking for the daughter lost. Too many years ago.

This didn't have the bare rolling look of the hills near the sea below San Francisco. There was more water here, rivers and lakes and forest country. I had flown into San Francisco as Travis McGee, taxied to a Holiday Inn near Fisherman's Wharf, and spent a day assembling a wardrobe to go with the new identity I had bought from a reliable source in Miami. The McGee identity fitted into a suitcase. I stored it and paid six months in advance. The storage receipt was the only link, and I didn't want it on me. Small things can be hidden in public places. There was a bank of new storage lockers in the bus station. They were not quite flush against the rear wall. I taped it at shoulder height to the back of the lockers, out of sight. If I could stand up, I could get it back. If I wanted it back.

9

I gave up walking when the heel of my right foot began to bother me. The work shoes were too heavy for one who had spent such a chunk of his life barefoot. I wished I had taken the bus.

I found a good place to hitch a ride. I hate to see the damn fools on the highways hitching in the wrong places. It is a waste of energy. You have to be where they can see you a long way off, and where you stand out well against the background. They have to be able to see a lot of highway beyond you, and they have to spot a place where they can pull off. You have to make a gesture at each car, a big sweeping one. You leave the duffel bag at your feet and you take your hat off, and you smile wide enough to show some teeth. An animal will roll onto his back to demonstrate his harmlessness. A man will grin. It is better to trust the animal.

A gaunt old man in a rattle-bang Ford pickup stopped at high noon and picked me up. He wore banker's clothes and a peaked cap that said Oakland Raiders.

"Only going as far as Lake Mendocino, friend," he said.

"Is that past Ukiah?"

"Next door. I can drop you off before I make my turn. Get in." He looked back, waiting for a hole in the traffic, and when one came along, he jumped into it with surprising acceleration.

"Don't know this country, eh?"

"Don't know it at all. This is the first time for me."

"Hunting work?"

"Well, I might have to do some to keep going. But mostly I'm trying to get some kind of trace of my little girl. I think she's out here somewhere."

"There's a lot of young girls out here somewhere. There was a time in the sixties when they'd come drifting up from San Francisco. Communes and farming and all. What they call alternative lifestyles. Potheads, mostly. No offense. I'm not saying your girl is one of those. She missing long?"

"Six years."

"Hear anything from her in all that time?"

"One time, and that was four years ago. She'll be

twenty now. Peg and me, we married young. Kathy was sixteen when we got those cards from her. They came over a month or so. They never gave an address we could write back to. They were mailed in San Francisco, and then the very last one was from Ukiah. It said she was joining up with some kind of church and we should forget about her forever. You know, when you've got just the one kid, you don't forget like that. It took the heart out of Peg. She died a while back, and after I sold off a little piece of land and the trailer and an old skiff, I thought I might as well use the money trying to find her."

"Friend, this state is chock-full of religions. You can find any kind you are looking for. There's some that'll take you to Guyana and teach you to raise oranges and how to kill yourself quick. They start in the north and go all the way down to the Mexican border, and to my way of thinking, the further south they go, the crazier they get. People are hunting around for something to believe in these days. All the stuff people used to believe in has kind of let them down hard. You'd have to know the name of the religion first, I'd say."

"I learned it by heart. The Church of the Apocrypha."

"I've lived pretty close to Ukiah for ten years, and I can't say I ever heard of it. But I've seen some strange ones drifting around the streets there, selling flowers and candy and wearing white robes."

"I can ask around there, I guess. Big place?"

"No. I'd guess maybe twelve thousand. What kind of work you do?"

"I fish commercial. Net work, mostly. Mullets usually. When they're hard to find, it pays good. When they're easy, it isn't hardly worthwhile going out, you get such small money. What kind of business are you in?"

"Investments."

"Oh." From the way he said it, I knew that was all I was going to learn. He moved the pickup right along, tailgating the people who wouldn't move over into the slow lane.

"Where would be a good place to ask in Ukiah?"

"Maybe the police. Police usually know about the crazies and where they live."

He dropped me off at the Ukiah ramp. The wind felt cool and fresh. I found one gas station that wouldn't let me use the rest room, and another one that would. I shaved off the stubble and put on my wire glasses and looked into the mirror. In the hard fluorescence, my deepwater tan looked yellowish. Deep grooves bracketed my mouth. The gold glasses did not give me a professorial look. I looked like a desert rat with bad eyes.

He was an officer of the law. Not too long ago he had been a fat, florid, hearty man. The balloon was deflating. He had made a couple of new holes in his belt. His color was bad. His chops sagged. He looked me over with a listless competence. And he listened to my story. "Apocrypha. Kind of rings a bell. Short dirty-white robes. Beards. Sister this and Brother that." He dialed a three-digit number and leaned back in his leather chair and began murmuring into the phone, listening for a time while he stared at the ceiling. Then he hung up and took a sheet of yellow paper and drew a crude map.

"Where that outfit was, McGraw, they were over in Lake County. They had a pretty good-sized tract. What you do, you take Twenty East and go over past Upper Lake, maybe two miles, and there's a little road heads off to the east, unpaved but a good surface. You go along that road, mostly uphill, and it winds around and there are little roads heading off it, smaller still, and that encampment is off at the end of one of those. You'll have to ask around."

"Thanks. I appreciate you taking the trouble."

"Afraid it won't help much. Seems they've pulled up and moved off someplace. Might be nobody left there at all."

"It's the only clue I've got."

For the moment he forgot his own woes. "Listen, McGraw. There's thousands of kids took off. A lot of them don't ever show again. It's a sign of the times. What I mean is, don't expect too much. It's a good thing to look around, to satisfy yourself you did all you could. But don't expect too much. Okay?"

"Thanks. I won't. I mean, I'll try not to."

By Sunday noon I had found it. I had spent the night in a small rental trailer under giant evergreens. I had hitched three rides, walked through two monstrous rainstorms, and climbed what seemed to be several mountains.

So now I stood where Gretel and her husband had stood. The signs were large and explicit. Red lettering on white. PRIVATE PROPERTY. NO TRESPASSING. The wire gate she had described blocked the road. Beyond the gate the road curved up and to the right, out of sight behind the trees and brush. There was a lean-to on the right, just beyond the gate. The last people I had asked, the ones who had given me the final directions, had said that they thought there were a few left up at the encampment, but that most of them had gone away. They said that sometimes they saw a van on the road. Black, with a gold cross painted on the sides.

I am Tom McGraw, looking for the traces of a daughter lost. I have a father's bullheaded determination. So I forge ahead. Climb the fence close to the gate, drop the duffel bag, and drop down beside it. Shoulder it and walk up the muddy road.

There was a cathedral of evergreens on either side of the road, standing at parade rest on the slope, the ground silent with needles. The sun was suddenly covered again, and I heard a high soft sigh of rainwind in the pine branches. I trudged up the curve and up a steeper pitch. The stand of trees dwindled, and there were boulders among them big as bungalows. I came out at the top. Far away to the northeast I could see sunlit mountains. I was on an old rocky plateau, quite level, as big as four football fields. It sloped gently down toward valleys and gullies on every side. Off to my right, at the end of the big plateau, was a clutter of small structures. The biggest was a corrugated steel and aluminum building that looked like a pre-fab warehouse. There were several small cement-block buildings, and several trailers on block foundations. I saw one derelict truck.

There was no sign of life. I wanted to see if the road continued on the other side of the field. I hollered and waited and heard no answer. I walked across and looked. There was no road down the slope. There had been a stand of small trees there, with the biggest about three inches in diameter. They were broken off about two feet above ground level. At first I thought somebody had driven up and down there with a vehicle. Something nagged at memory. I walked down the slope. The damage was not fresh. The wood was splintered and dry. I squatted and found where slugs had creased the bark. Very heavy sustained fire from an automatic weapon would chew them off just like that. Using the bark creases for rough triangulation, I was able to go back up the slope to the approximate area where the weapon had been. I poked around and finally saw a glint of metal in a crack of the rock. I levered it out with a twig. It was a white metal shell casing, center-fire, in a smaller caliber than I would have expected. But it looked as if there was room for a hefty load of propellant. There was an unfamiliar symbol on the end of it, like a figure 4 open at the top, and with an extra horizontal line across the upright.

I tossed it up and caught it and put it in my pocket. A strange exercise for a church group, shooting down a young forest. And then picking up all the shell casings.

I headed toward the buildings, but before I reached them I heard, coming toward me, the sound of a lot of footsteps, running almost in unison. They burst up a slope and onto the plateau about fifty yards away from me. Seven of them in single file, weapons slung, left hands holding the weapons, right arms swinging. I had the impression of great fitness and great effort. They were young. They wore gray-green coveralls, fatigue caps, ammo belts, and backpacks. One of them saw me and yelled something. With no hesitation they stopped and ran back, spreading into combat patrol interval, spinning, falling prone, right at the dropoff line, seven muzzles aimed at me. I shed the duffel bag and held my arms high.

"Hey!" I yelled. "Hey, what's the matter?"

"Down," a voice yelled. "Face down, spread-eagle. Now!"

Once down, I peered up and saw two walking toward me, weapons still ready, while two others were heading for the buildings, running in a crouching zigzag, in the event I had come with friends.

Hands patted me. I was told to shut up. I was told to roll over. One stood over me, muzzle at my forehead, and I suddenly realized she was female. The other, a man with a drooping mustache, did the frisking.

"Now what the hell are you doing here?" he demanded. "How did you get here? What did you do to Nicky?"

"The way I got here, I walked. I didn't see any Nicky."

"You come past the gate?"

"Yes."

"Can't you read? Didn't you see the signs?"

"I saw them. But I had to come up here and talk to somebody about my little girl. She joined up here. Maybe you know her. Kathy McGraw? I'm her daddy, Tom McGraw."

"Oh, for God's sake," the man said. The girl didn't relax her weapon.

"Can I get up?"

"Shut up," the girl said. "What are you going to do, Chuck?"

"What the hell *can* we do? Put him in C Building and wait for Pers to get back."

The girl gasped and said, "Oh, Jesus! Look at what's coming, Chuck."

A huge young blond man was coming across the field, carrying a fair-sized dead buck across his shoulders.

"God damn you, Nicky, why'd you leave the gate?"

He approached and eased the deer to the ground, rolled his shoulders to loosen them. "And this man came in, huh? Oh, great! I ought to kick you loose from your head, fellow."

"You're the one should be kicked, Nicky," the girl said.

"That sucker came right out onto the road and looked at me and ran back in. I shot too fast and missed and gutshot him, and you can't leave an animal go running off like that. I followed him a mile and a half, fast as I could go. What'd you expect me to do, Nena? I killed him, gutted him, and brought him in."

"It isn't what *I* expect you to do," she said. "It's what Brother Persival expects."

"You can get up," Chuck said.

After I stood up, I looked at Nicky. His face was troubled. "Boring damn duty," he said. "Hang around down there eight hours at a time. Nobody ever comes. And then when you leave for a couple minutes, some damn fool climbs the fence."

"He's hunting his daughter. She used to be here," Chuck said.

"What was her name?" Nena asked me. She appeared to be in her early twenties. Olive skin, slender face, very dark eyes. She had that excess of bursting health which gives the whites of the eyes a bluish tint. No makeup. The long dense black lashes were her own.

"Katherine McGraw. She'd be twenty years old by now. Reddish-brown hair and blue eyes and some freckles when she was younger. Maybe they went away."

"Got a picture of her?"

"The best picture we had of her, it was when she was thirteen, and after Peg died, that was my wife, damn if I could find it. I looked all over for that picture. She was a pretty child. She ought to be a good-looking woman. Her ma was."

"You don't know what new name she took?"

"She never said. In those postcards."

"I can't help you. I don't know if anybody can—or wants to, Mr. McGraw. People that join up don't go back to the lives they had before."

"Where did everybody go from here?" I asked.

No answer. They urged me along and shut me up in C Building. It was a cement-block building about ten feet square, with two windows with heavy wire mesh over them. There was a wooden chair, a tree-trunk table, a stained mattress on the floor, and a forty-watt bulb hanging from a cord from the middle of the ceiling. There was a ragged pile of religious comic books, a musty army blanket, a two-quart jug of tepid drinking water, and a bucket to use as a toilet. They had taken my belt, shoelaces, and duffel bag. The door was solidly locked. I heard some bird sounds, and that was all. I wondered if they had all left.

Darkness came, and there was a quick light rain on the corrugated roof of my prison. I heard a distant motor noise and tried to decide if it was coming or going. When the sound did not change, I realized it might be a generator, the engine turning over at an unchanging rpm. So I tried my light bulb again, and it went on. It did not help the decor.

Two of them came and unlocked my door. They had a dazzling-bright gasoline lantern, an automatic weapon at the ready, and a tin bowl full of stew. They were two I had glimpsed before at a distance. One was a sallow blond girl with very little chin, and the other was a young man with an Asian cast to his features.

No harm to object. After all, I was Tom McGraw. "Why are you people pointing guns at me all the time? Damn it, I'm not some kind of criminal. I don't like being locked up like this. Where's my stuff you took away from me? I got my rights. You people are all gun-happy."

"Shut up, Dads," the Oriental said, and they closed the door and locked it.

Even though I had to eat it with a little white plastic spoon, I found the venison stew delicious. And it had been a long time since I had enjoyed the taste of anything. The lack of interest in eating had leaned me down a little over the past weeks.

There was a cook in the camp. Even a slight taste of wine in the stew. Boiled onions, carrots, celery, tomatoes. And a lot of it. After my dinner I read a religious comic book. All about Samson yanking down that temple. Samson looked like Burt Reynolds. Delilah looked like Liz Taylor. The temple looked like the Chase Bank.

After I turned my light off, I stretched out in my clothes on the dingy mattress and covered myself with the musty sheet. And in the darkness, I went over what I knew. I followed Meyer's injunction. Never mix up what you really know with what you think you know. Don't let speculation water down the proven truths. Leap to conclusions only when that is the only way to safety.

People talking outside my door awakened me. I knew it was late. I realized it was just the changing of the guard. I heard the clink of metal and a yawning good night and went back to sleep.

In the morning I was escorted down to a rushing tumbling icy creek by Nicky and the chinless blonde. She carried the weapon. I carried the soil bucket in one hand and held up my trousers with the other. I had asked politely for my belt, and they told me to shut up. They pointed me to the place on the bank where I could wash out the bucket in the fast water. Then I was allowed to go upstream to a place where I could dash some of the icy water into my face. Big Nicky was sullen. The blonde was trying to cheer him. When he answered, I found out her name was Stella. So I had four names out of the group of eight. They marched me back to C Building, again carrying the bucket, now empty, and holding up my trousers. I asked when they expected Mr. Persival, and they told me to shut up.

An hour later I was given cold scrambled eggs and cold toast on a pie tin, with another plastic spoon. They had changed cooks.

At midmorning I saw an interesting tableau from my window. I do not think they realized that I could see it. I had to get my face close to the screen and look slantwise. Two couples. Nena and a young man. Stella and a young man. Out of uniform. Casual clothes. Each carried luggage. Suitcase, or small bedroll or duffel bag. Chuck stood off to one side, watching them closely. He had a whistle in his mouth and what was apparently a stopwatch in his hand. I could not understand the instructions he yelled at them. They walked close and lovingly, laughing and talking together, looking at each other, not at their surroundings. When the whistle blew, they would snatch at the luggage, yank it open, remove an automatic weapon, let the luggage fall to the ground, stand with their backs to each other, leaning against each other, almost, in a little deadly square formation, hold the weapons aiming out in four directions, and revolve slowly.

Then they would repack and do it again. I think

I watched fifteen rehearsals. Their time improved noticeably. I guessed that they had it down to just about four seconds before Chuck ended the exercise. Four seconds to change from two couples, lounging along, laughing together, to an engine of destruction.

I disobeyed one of Meyer's rules. I made an assumption or two. I assumed that they planned to put on their little act in a crowded place, like an airport or a shopping plaza, and the guns would be loaded, and people would be blown apart while still caught up in a horror of disbelief.

But why? They worked so very hard at it. They seemed so dedicated and intent. These were bright young people, very fit and disciplined. Playing a strange, strange game.

The noon meal was more venison stew. Still tasty.

The black van arrived in the late afternoon. It passed my window before I could see anyone in it. But I saw the gold cross painted on the side.

At least twenty minutes passed before my door was unlocked. Chuck said, "Strip and pile everything on the floor right in front of the door here. Fold it and pile it. Everything."

"Damn it all, I want to know why I'm—"

"Look. This is an order and it's serious. You want to strip, or be stripped?"

I did as I was told. They backed me into a corner and inspected the room to see if there was anything of mine hidden in it. That search didn't take long. They went off with everything.

It could have been an hour later before anybody came near me. Then it was Mr. Persival himself. A tall stooped figure, shaggy tousled dark hair flecked with gray. Long face and a lantern jaw. Eyes set deep in the bony sockets. The sports clothes looked unlikely on him, as did the big glasses with the slight amber tint, the boldface watch, water resistant to three hundred feet. He was an actor playing a contemporary Lincoln, or a Vermont storekeeper who'd built one store into a chain. He walked with care, the way the ill walk. The girl called Nena slid into the room with her weapon aimed at my chest and moved over to the side to keep Persival out of the line of fire. She was lithe and quick.

"My name is Persival, Mr. McGraw." A deep voice, soft and gentle. An air of total command, total assurance. "My young associates and I would be grateful for some explanation of this."

He held out a big slow hand, and resting on the palm was the cartridge case I had picked up. I spoke without hesitation, blessing the Susan I had known long ago for teaching me how to live a part. "Explanation? I picked that up out there. I never saw one just like it. I put it in my pocket. I mean, if that's the same one."

"I think we will go outside and you will show me where you found it."

"Can I have some clothes?"

"It isn't that chilly yet."

When I hesitated, I saw Nena lower the aiming point from chest to belly. I couldn't read anything in her eyes. She walked behind us. Persival walked just out of arm's reach, off to my left.

"And what were you doing over here?"

"I was looking for somebody so I could ask them about the Church of the Apocrypha, Mr. Persival. I wondered if the road I came up went down this side to more buildings, maybe. Then I saw all those trees down there, the way they were busted off at the same height. I went down and looked at them. I saw trees looking like that after we cleared some people out who were trying to ambush us, but the man on point stopped them in time. It was done some time ago. Weeks ago, probably, from the dead leaves and the dry wood. I saw slug marks on the trunk and I could kind of figure where the weapon must have been. Or weapons. Right over here. So I saw a glint in a crack in the rocks. Here, I think. No, it was this one. Because here is the twig I hooked it out with. It was a kind I never saw before, so I put it in my pocket. And now you've got it."

He nodded at me and smiled in a kindly way. "You were just wandering around here, Mr. McGraw?"

"Looking for somebody to talk to."

He sighed and said, "Yes. Looking for somebody to talk to."

"Then I was walking toward the buildings when the patrol came up onto the flat right over there."

"Why do you call it a patrol?"

"I don't know. People in uniform carrying weapons and ammo, wearing light packs. Not enough for a squad, and they were coming back out of the country. What would you call them?"

"Followers of the true faith."

"Well, I wouldn't know that. I would like to know something about my little girl and how I can find her."

"Let's walk back. It's getting chilly."

"I'd appreciate that," I said. If there is any way to feel more naked than standing out in 60-degree weather as the day is ending, with a girl aiming an automatic weapon at the small of your back, I would not care to hear of it.

On the way back I noticed that he did not walk quite as far out to my left. I could have reached him, if I felt suicidal.

"You were carrying a considerable amount of cash in the double lining of that duffel bag, Mr. McGraw."

"I was hoping you wouldn't look that close."

"We're very careful people. Is it stolen?"

"Hell, no, it's not stolen! Or maybe it is now, hah?"

"Don't become agitated, please. Just tell me

where you got it." I told him. He thought it over and nodded. "So you decided to make your funds last as long as possible, so your search would not be hampered by the need to seek employment."

"That's exactly correct."

We went inside. He sat on the straight chair and told the girl to go get my clothes. She hesitated, and he looked stonily at her and said, "Sister?" She scuttled away. She brought the clothing. Persival sent her away. He watched me dress. He said, "You seem to have suffered an extraordinary number of wounds, Mr. McGraw. Are they all service-connected?"

"No, sir, not all. Two are. High on my back on the right side and the shoulder. And here on the left hip."

"How about that huge wound on your right thigh?"

"That was a hunting accident long ago. I went a long time before they found me. It got infected, and I was out of my head and nearly died. Some of this other stuff, I'm in kind of an active line of work. And the guys I work with, when we play we play rough. Beside that, sir, I have a bad temper sometimes. I go out of my head, sort of. I haven't kilt anybody, but I've tried hard."

"You don't seem to have the hands of a commercial fisherman."

I held my hands out and looked at them, backs and fronts. "What do you mean? Oh, you mean like

145

those old boys that go out in the freezing water off of Maine or someplace? They get those big paws like catcher's mitts, and those busted twisted fingers. My daddy had hands like that from working the big nets. It's all nylon now, and you have to wear tough gloves or cut yourself to ribbons. Besides, I haven't been out working the nets for a long time now."

"You seem to be in excellent shape, Mr. McGraw."

"I'm not as good as I'd like to be. You know, the old wind. And the legs give out first. But I've always stayed in pretty good shape. Never had a beer belly."

"And you have had combat experience?"

"As a grunt. I can do the BAR, mortars, flame, mines, whatever. I was in it fourteen months. Got to be a utility infielder."

"Then you must have watched our little . . . patrol with a practiced eye. Would you have any comment?"

"I haven't seen much. They're trained down fine, physically. They move quick and they move well. They carry the weapons at the ready. But all the rest of it? I don't know what they can do. They look good. What are they training up to do anyway?"

"Please sit down there, on the mattress, Mr. McGraw. Make yourself comfortable." He hitched the straight chair closer and leaned over, forearms resting on his knees, long fingers dangling. "I will do you the courtesy of speaking to you with absolute frankness."

"Something happened to my little girl?"

"Please. I wouldn't know about that, nor even how I could find out. I am trying to tell you that if I were to follow my own rules, I would have my young associates take you out into the tall trees and blow your head off."

"Why? Why the hell would you do that?"

"You came stumbling and bumbling in here through an entrance that should have been guarded. The young man responsible will be punished. But I am not taking pity on your innocence and your naïve quest. I am thinking of sparing you only because I believe there is some specific use I can make of you."

"Such as what?"

"Are you in any position to ask me that, right now?"

"I reckon not, if you don't want me to, Mr. Persival."

It was getting so dark I could hardly see his face. I could see a pale reflection of the after-dusk sky in his tinted glasses. He had a strange weight and force about him. Total confidence and a total impartiality.

The distant engine started. The overhead bulb flickered, glowed, brightened. He stood up and stared down at me, then turned on his heel and left, leaving the door open. I walked out and stood with my thumbs hooked in my belt, looking at the faint glow in the western sky, above the sharp tips of the big pines far down the slope. I had the feeling I was being watched, and that it had been set up before Persival paid his call. I yawned and stretched, scratched myself, and slouched back into C Building, wondering if I should have pushed the money question a little harder. Would Tom McGraw have pushed it? Not when faced with the possibility of getting shot in the head.

I wondered when they were going to bring me something to eat, and if it would be the stew again.

Then I heard them all coming. They had flashlights and lanterns. I tightened up, and then heard laughter.

The sallow blonde arrived first, carrying a camp stool and a cooking pot and a flashlight. "We're having a party, Brother Thomas! At *your* house!"

"So come right in, Sister Stella. Come right in," I said.

10

They filled the room. They brought stools and cushions, a gasoline lantern, food, and wine. Nine of them and one of me. Plastic paper plates and genuine forks. Paper cups and a big container of coffee. Jolly and smiling. I knew Chuck, the patrol leader, and three of his six soldiers—Nena and Stella and the Oriental. I learned that the Oriental was Sammy. The other three were Haris, a slender blond Englishman—the name pronounced to rhyme with police—and Barry, a young black with a shaved head and dusty tan coloring, and Ahman, who looked like a young Turkish pirate. Persival was there, and also Alvor, one I had not seen before. He was chunky, with a broad gray heavy face, colorless eyes and lips, mouse hair, and huge shoulders. I made certain I got all the names right. Alvor had to have been in the van with Persival. Nicky was missing, and I overheard a comment that indicated he was down at the gate as a lookout.

I was sitting on the narrow mattress, leaning back against a cushion, with Nena and Stella on either side of me. I was the center of all attention. When I remarked that it had certainly seemed like a very strange Christmas day, they reacted as if I had said something profound and witty. We had Christmas toasts in a sharp California red. I was being touched by the young women beside me, not in any sensuous way, but with little pats of affection, of liking. And when the men would squat in front of me to talk directly to me, they would slap me on the side of the leg, give my ankle a squeeze. Wherever I looked there was someone maintaining direct eye contact with me, projecting warm approval. I tucked McGee's suspicions into the back of my mind. Brother Tom McGraw was a lonely man, of lonely habits. So I responded to warmth. And to flattery.

"I knew at once you are a highly intelligent and sensitive man, Mr. McGraw," Persival said. "I could sense that about you. But you seem to feel the need to conceal the real you from the outside world. We are not like that here. We're together."

"In school I never got past—"

"Public education in this country means less than

nothing," Sammy said. "From the earliest grades, the children are taught to conform, to be good consumers, to have no interest in their government or the structure of their society. The rebels drop out. The rich get classified as exceptional students and go on to the schools which teach them how to run the world, their world. Never apologize for dropping out, Brother."

The stew was beef this time. I said it was great. Haris, the Englishman, had cooked it. "Whatever there is, we share. Always," he said.

"You're a worker," Nena told me. "You have a skill. You use your skill to feed the people. Even though you are exploited, it's still something to be proud of."

Mr. Persival said, with poetry and force, "We can guess that there have been Christmas nights like this in mountain country all over the world, little groups of determined people, meeting together, all of them willing to give their lives for their beliefs. In the Cuban mountains. In the mountains of Honduras. Mexico, Yugoslavia, Chile, Peru, Rhodesia. Together, sharing, living the great dream."

"What's the dream?" I asked.

"The same as yours, of course," said Persival. "Freedom for all people of all colors. An end to imperialist exploitation. To each according to his needs. You are the kind of man who, once committed, would give his life for what he believes."

"I've been known as stubborn. I don't give up easy. But what you were saying there, sir, isn't that kind of Commie?"

He shook his head sadly. "Communist, Socialist, humanist, Christian Democrat, Liberation Army. The tags mean less than nothing, Brother Thomas. We do God's work. We are the militant arm of the Church of the Apocrypha. We are the ones who have been tested. We work for mankind against the exploiters, deceivers, the criminal warmongers. We will win if we have to tear down the entire structure of society. Your daughter believed in the cause or she wouldn't have joined us."

"She wasn't much for destroying things."

"Most of the people in the Church are gentle people. We are the elite. We're pleased with you, Brother Thomas. We may have a mission for you."

It was at that point I began to feel very strange. At first I thought it was because the room was airless, even with the door standing wide open. Colors got brighter. People's faces began to bulge and shrink, bulge and shrink. My tongue thickened. They had popped me with something. It turned the world into fun-house mirrors. And I knew it could give me a better chance of getting my head blown apart. I made my tongue sound thicker than it was. I began to do as much inconspicuous hyperventilation as I could manage. More oxygen never hurt anything. I crawled across to the water jug, sat and upended it and drank heavily, and crawled back. I tipped over my wine by accident and held my glass out for more.

By then we were into recitations of training, with the freedom fighters standing up and declaiming their background.

Nena stood very straight and said in a parade-ground voice, "Basic training at Kochovskaya. Guerrilla training at Simferopol. Selected by World Federation of Democratic Youth in Budapest. Transport arranged by World Federal Trade Unions in Prague."

When she sat down everyone applauded. Ahman stood up and said, "Basic and guerrilla training PLO Camp Three in Jordan and Camp Nine in Lebanon. Graduate, University of Maryland." Applause.

Barry had been trained in Cuba by the DGI and had been a weapons instructor at Baninah near Benghazi in Libya. Chuck had trained at a camp near Al-Ghaidha in South Yemen, along with people from the IRA. Sammy had trained in the U.S. Marine Corps and later in the Cuban training center near Bagdad, where the famous Carlos was an adviser. Persival interrupted to give Carlos's correct name, Ilyich Rameirez Sanchez. Stella had been in the Weather Underground and had trained in their mountain camp in Oregon, and later in Bulgaria.

"How," I said heavily, "how these great people get to go so many crazy places inna worl' anyhow?"

"We selected them, Brother Thomas. We tested them, and we selected them, and we sent them away to be trained and come back to us. We sent them as delegates, most of them, to the World Peace Council meetings in Helsinki, or the World Federation of Democratic Youth in Budapest. You see only a few here. There are scores of them, Brother Thomas. Travel is easily arranged for them. The Church provides the funds, of course. They are pledged to make this a better world. They are saviors of mankind."

I mumbled something unintelligible and slowly toppled over to my left to land with my head in Stella's lap, eyes closed, breathing slowly and heavily. I hoped the show would continue. I wanted to hear more. But my collapse broke it up. They picked up all their gear and the dishes and left, after covering me up and turning out the light. I heard the locking of my door. My head was still thick with whatever it was they had given me. I did some fast pushups in the darkness, and a series of knee bends. My knees creaked and breath came fast. But it helped a little. I slept heavily.

I awakened once before daylight and did not know where I was. It alarmed me. Then I remembered. And I remembered the way Gretel and I had talked about what to do on our first Christmas together. We had decided to take the *Flush* down to the lower end of Biscayne Bay and find a protected anchorage with maximum privacy and swim, and eat, and drink, and exchange Christmas greetings all day long.

No breakfast arrived. I pounded on the door and did some yelling. At about ten o'clock they unlocked the door and shoved Nicky in, with such force that he ran across the room and smacked the cement wall with his palms. He had a purple cheek, with the right eye swollen almost shut.

He sat in the chair and slumped over, staring at the floor.

"What's going on?" I asked him.

"Damn bastards are all uptight. Do it by the book. No variations permitted. According to them, I've fucked up twice in a row, which is twice too many times, but they won't even listen. One lousy weapon. One lousy Czech machine pistol, and I forgot to clean it after it was in the creek. For Chrissake, they've got a whole damn building full of weapons, grenades, plastique, nitro, napalm, and God only knows what else. One rotten pistol." He peered up at me with his good eye. "You fucked up too, eh? Or you wouldn't be locked in."

"I did? I don't know how. I got a little drunk."

"Persival doesn't think you're who you say you are, so they were going to give you some love-buzzing and open you up some, and then try some kind of Pentothal stuff he uses. You must have slipped up. Who the hell are you anyway?"

"Thomas McGraw, dammit! Looking for my girl, dammit! Are you crazy or something? I *like* all your friends. I don't know why they locked me up again. It don't make sense."

"You must have slipped up, or you wouldn't be here. That's all I know. Except I know I slipped up once too often. The way I am, when there's no action, I relax. I can't stay wound up all the time. These characters are gung-ho every minute. Like a bunch of cheerleaders. You *like* them, huh? Because they spent the evening liking you. That's the way it works. Barry, Sammy, and Ahman have had some action. Not much. Chicken-shit operations. Car bombs and burn-downs. In and out, like thieves. I had time in Nam, and then Zambia. We were in the hills near Refunsa. The way it worked, the Zambians would cross into Rhodesia and hit and run, and then suck the Rhodesian army units into Zambia, and we'd ambush them. Very tough people. Very tough country. I just can't stand waiting around so long with no action. I get sloppy. Persival says we don't move until maybe summer. Coordinated. You never get to know much. You hear there are fifteen groups and then you hear forty. Who knows? When it comes time, we'll get the word from Sister Elena Marie."

"Who?"

"I forgot you don't know. The boss lady. They send out cassettes. I don't believe in a lot of this stuff, but I believe in her. I believe in her all the way." His voice and face were solemn.

There were questions I wanted to ask, but they

were not questions Tom McGraw would have asked.

"Do you think this Sister Elena Marie would know where my little girl is?"

"I don't know. I don't even know if they've got any central records. I don't know where *she* is, even, where she makes the tapes. They say there were like three hundred of them here at one time, and this was a small retreat compared to the others. They moved them out to where they could help raise the money. Everybody has to do that. Your daughter had to do it too. Teams go up and down the streets, hitting every house. Sometimes you say it's for children, and sometimes for foreign missions. You sell stuff. Handicraft stuff. Also candy and artificial flowers and maybe fresh-baked bread. Once you catch on, it isn't hard. Four on our team, we'd raise two hundred, three hundred a day, every day. Ride around in the black vans with the crosses. Twenty cents' worth of junk candy for two dollars, to help the starving Christian children in Lebanon. You can claim one quarter of what your team raised when you have to stand up in the meeting and shout out what you turned in. They switch the teams around a lot. I'm so big people were always glad I was on their team. It's harder to say no to big people."

The door opened again. Four of them were there. Ahman and Sammy were in their coveralls, carrying the automatic weapons, left hands clamped on the forestock, right hands around the trigger assembly, long curved clips in place. Persival looked unlikely in an orange-yellow leisure suit and white turtleneck. Stone-faced, no-color, big-shouldered Alvor wore a wrinkled dark business suit, a white shirt with a frayed collar, and a narrow striped tie.

"Come along," Persival ordered. The four of them walked a dozen feet behind us. Persival told us where to go. We went to the place where the flats sloped down to the splintered trees, near the spot where I had found the cartridge case.

"Stop there," he said. "Move to your right two steps, McGraw. Now both of you turn slowly around and face me."

My heart gave an extra thump. Ahman and Sammy were aiming the weapons at us. Sammy was holding on Nick, and Ahman on me. Ahman's swarthy face and shiny black eyes revealed nothing. So maybe, when Persival had told somebody to check me out, they had checked more carefully than I had assumed they would, and found that Thomas McGraw had been dead for some time, and never had a daughter.

"What the hell is the matter with you people now?" I asked. I did not have to fake a definite quaver in my voice.

"You know, each of you, why you are dying today."

"Chicken shit," Nicky said in a husky voice.

"There can be *no* carelessness. *None*. Maximum

precautions will be taken to prevent any premature disclosure. There will be no second chance for anyone whose actions could compromise us all. All orders will be obeyed, without question, without argument."

"Chicken shit," Nicky said again.

"Come here, Mr. McGraw," Persival said. "Over here. Stop there. Fine. Now turn and face the condemned." I was three feet from Persival, but I noted as I turned that Ahman's gun muzzle followed me like an empty steel eye socket.

Persival's voice deepened. "Dear God of wrath and mercy, take unto thy bosom this soldier of our faith and grant him eternal peace. We send him to thee now so that he will not further endanger the holy mission with which thou hast entrusted us, thy faithful soldiers in the army of justice. Amen.

His hand appeared in front of me, holding a slender automatic pistol with a long barrel. "Take it and shoot him in the head, please," Persival said. Same tone of voice as he would have said, "Have some more stew, please."

And the scenario was suddenly clear. I would shoot Nicky in the head with a blank, and my obedience would remove Persival's lingering suspicion of me, and Nicky would be frightened into being more careful next time. Two birds with one fake stone.

"It's ready to go," he said. "Just aim and fire."

There was no great need to aim. Nicky was per-

haps fifteen feet from me. If you aim a handgun
with the same motion you use to point your finger
at someone, if the barrel becomes your finger, you
can hit a six-inch circle on the other side of the
room ninety-nine out of a hundred times.

So I pointed and fired. It made an unimportant
snapping sound. A dark spot appeared beside
Nicky's nose, on his good cheek. It snapped his
head back a little. He made a coughing sound and
sagged down onto one knee, then rolled over backward and rolled down the slope. I moved forward
to keep him in sight. He came to rest in dead
branches, against a splintered trunk, his back to us.
One leg jumped and quivered and vibrated for a
few seconds and then subsided. He seemed to become visibly smaller.

The life had gone out of him, now and forever.
Persival reached around and tugged the weapon out
of my hand and moved back away from me. "Turn
around slowly," he said. This was not the scenario I
had envisioned. I had imagined all of them crowd-
ing around me, Nicky included, whacking me on
the back, welcoming me to the team.

Instead, Persival was chunking a magazine into
the pistol. The slide had remained back after I had
fired. So there had been just the one shell in the
chamber. This man took no chances. They held
weapons on me. Ahman had set his weapon aside
and was collapsing an SX-70 Polaroid while
Sammy examined the print as it developed. I re-

called hearing that tantalizingly familiar sound of the SX-70 a fraction of a second after I had fired and killed Nicky.

They were all curious about me, all waiting for my reaction. I could read a certain righteous satisfaction on their faces. I was fighting nausea and hoping I hadn't turned so gray-green they would suspect how close I was. Nausea, and a tendency of the world around me to fade in and out. Killing is such an ancient taboo. Only freaks ever adjust to killing people they have known and talked to, except when it is to save their own lives. Discipline enables uniformed people to kill unseen strangers. Children can imitate something seen on television, but the aftershock can be deadly. I had killed before, and it has never ceased being a wrenching psychic trauma. As I sought for some reaction which would make me reasonably acceptable to these people, suddenly I lost control of my acquired identity.

I stared at Persival. He was trickery. He was death. He was insane devotion to an incomprehensible cause. He was a shooter of little silver pellets into the necks of the lovely and innocent.

"You dirty, murderous, crazy son of a bitch!" I said in a low and shaky voice.

He raised the reloaded weapon and aimed carefully from eight feet away at a spot on my forehead. I knew where the slug would strike. The spot felt round and icy.

I was convinced I was about to join Nicky. He knew he was going to die, and I could find no better last words than his.

"Chicken shit," I said.

"Any questions, McGraw?"

"There's nothing I want to know that you can answer." I was watching the trigger finger. As soon as I saw pressure whiten it, I was going to dive for his ankles and try to come up with the weapon before Sammy and Ahman could blow me away.

"Any last statement, fisherman?"

"I will state that if you don't make the first shot good, I'll get my hands on you before you can fire that thing again."

He looked at me for a long time, and then slowly lifted the barrel of the weapon until it pointed at the sky.

"I think my first hunch was correct, Brother Thomas. I think we can train you and find a use for you. I think you can become very valuable."

I could feel the tension go out of all of us. Deep exhalations.

He put the weapon away. He turned to Sammy and reached for the picture. After Persival had examined it, he motioned me closer and handed it to me. I was on the right, in fuzzy focus, enough of the left side of my face showing to make me recognizable. The barrel of the pistol was half raised to the perpendicular, the ineradicable habit pattern of people used to firing pistols and revolvers. Nick was near the left margin of the print, in sharp focus. He was going down, but his knee had not yet touched. His head was tilted back from impact, with the tiny death mark visible next to his nose.

Handing it back, I said, "Is this some kind of leverage?"

"It is, Brother Thomas, but not the way you think. Call it a verification of my instinct, useful when I go after permission for what I have in mind."

"I don't know what you mean."

"Ahmar, arrange burial. Full roster except, of course, for Barry down on the gate. Have Haris read the service. I am going for a walk with Mr. McGraw."

11

Persival did not walk well. He moved slowly and seemed to have trouble with his balance. The sky was turning gray, and the wind was cooler. We walked to the end of the small plateau. He seated himself on the trunk of a large pine which had fallen at the edge of the slope.

He lowered himself carefully. With a wry Lincolnesque smile he said, "I have what the young call bad wheels. I was the guest for a memorable period of time of an amiable old party named Somoza. He had my legs broken."

I sat astride the log about eight feet from him. "This," he said, "is the ancient definition of the best kind of education, the pupil on one end of a log and the teacher on the other."

"What do I—"

He stopped me with a raised hand. "Just let me ramble a bit. Answer me when I ask you a question. You would seem to know small boats and know the sea. And with your background, no one would question your interest in purchasing a certain sort of small boat."

"I don't want to use my search money for a boat."

"You are talking trivia, and when you do, you bore me."

"I came here to find my kid. Maybe that's boring to you, but it's not to me."

"McGraw, you are going to have to learn how to accept discipline."

"Mr. Persival, you can't run me the same way you run those people of yours. I'll answer you when you ask questions, and I'll answer the questions you don't ask. I talk when I please."

He looked me over. He was patently exasperated.

"Brother Thomas, can you swim?"

"Yes."

"I'm glad to hear that. A lot of commercial fishermen can't. Do you know how to use scuba gear?"

"Yes."

"Do you know what a limpet mine is?"

"Yes."

"Can you tell me? I want to be sure you know."

"It's a mine that sticks to what it is going to blow up. It can be magnetic, or covered with stickum. It can have a timer or be blown up by a transmitter."

"Very good! You've worked around explosive charges?"

"Enough to be careful."

"Suppose I gave you the task of fastening a limpet mine to the hull of one of those new tankers which carry frozen liquefied gas. How would you go about it?"

I recalled what he had said about the boat purchase. It was enough of a clue. "In the area where the tanker is, I'd get hold of a commercial fishing boat, small. One-man operation, with an inboard or outboard. I'd dress right for the climate and the place. I'd fish the area, catch fish, sell the catch. I'd keep track of the winds and tides, and when everything was right, I'd have a breakdown and get carried up against the hull of the ship, maybe forward where the flare would hide me from the weather decks. Maybe if I had a little electric outboard let down through the hull, and concealed somehow, I could count on drifting to exactly where I would have to be. The breakdown should be about dusk. I'd place the mine, arm it, then get my breakdown fixed and get out of there."

"Suppose you were stopped and searched by a harbor patrol?"

"I could explain the electric outboard. The limpet would have to look like something else."

"Such as?"

I shrugged. "Maybe a mushroom anchor, threaded so you could unscrew the shank."

I could see that he liked that. "I believe I was right in deciding we can find a use for you, Brother McGraw."

"Not blowing up a ship. I won't do that."

"Whether or not you will do it or won't do it is not the point at issue right now. It would be a considerable time in the future. Things can be worked out, I'm sure."

And I could certainly guess how they'd be worked out. I had been wrong about Nicky. But this was a certainty. The little limpet mine would have a trigger and a timing device and there would be careful instruction on how to set it. But the act of placing it against metal would activate it. I wasn't one of the true believers. I was expendable.

"I don't hold with killing people that never did anything to me. That's terrorism."

"Terrorism? Beware of tag words. General Sherman was a terrorist. The Continental Congress was a terrorist society. How about Pancho Villa, air strikes on cities, the torpedoing of ocean liners? Beware of semantics."

I played dumb. "What do you mean? I've got nothing against the Jews."

"Semantics, Brother, not Semitics. The study of words. In World War Two, the Londoners worshiped their heroic young men who risked heavy flak to drop bombs on Germany and despised the degenerate fiends in human form who flew over, risking heavy flak, to drop bombs on English cities. Begin calls Arafat a terrorist. Begin led a squad which blew up a British hotel, killing scores of people, when he was a young so-called terrorist."

A light rain began to fall, steeply slanted by the increasing wind. Persival got up. "We'll go into all this, Brother Thomas, after you have a chance to hear Sister Elena Marie and think about the message she brings us. Incidentally, you will have been moved by now into one of the travel trailers. T-Six. The green-and-white one. You'll be much more comfortable."

"Is it okay to ask if I can have my money back now?"

"No. It isn't acceptable to ask at this time."

"Do you know when I can ask, Mr. Persival?"

"You will be told. Every effort is being made to locate your daughter. I want you to know that. While you are here, records are being searched."

We were walking back in the light rain, at his pace.

"Is it okay to mention I never had breakfast this morning?"

"You have the run of the place, Brother. Stay up on the flats. Do not head down the hill at any point. I am sure you can locate the kitchen."

A small group was straggling ahead of us toward the buildings. Chuck, Nena, Stella, Sammy, Haris,

Ahman, and Alvor, all but Alvor in the short white robes which looked like smocks except for the monk's hoods attached to them. The women and Haris wore the hoods pulled up, and Haris carried a book.

"I see the service is over," Persival said.

"They dig a fast grave."

"It was all prepared," he said. He smiled at me in a fatherly way. He laid his hand on my shoulder. "Actually, Brother, there were two. Just in case."

"In case I couldn't shoot him?"

He took his hand away. "Let's say it was just in case."

I checked out my green-and-white travel trailer. It was an old Scottie, sitting on cement blocks. It had recently been cleaned. There were some water droplets on the flat surfaces. There were two folded blankets, no sheets. There was a tiny gas heater, a hand-pumped water supply and a Porta-Potty. My duffel bag was on the foot of the bed. There was no way to lock it. I had the uneasy feeling that Nicky had lived here in this constricted space, had curled his long bulk on the bed that was built across the rear end of the trailer. I kept seeing that Polaroid shot. It was curiously more vivid than what I had actually seen.

I went looking for the kitchen. The steel warehouse building was tightly secured. I came upon Alvor and asked him. He did not answer. He merely pointed. It was the only frame building in the group of structures, about twelve feet by twenty, with unfinished open studding on the inside. There was a kerosene stove, an old kerosene refrigerator, two plank tables on sawhorses, and some unmatched chairs and camp stools. The utensils and plates and cups were on open shelves made of planks and bricks. There was a big blackboard at the other end of the room.

I found butter and eggs, scrambled four eggs, and sat at the plank table and ate them. Barry came in, relieved of guard duty, and smiled at me. "Got everything you need, Brother?"

"This is fine, thanks."

"Want some coffee?"

"Thanks, yes."

He brought it over, as well as a cup for himself. and sat across from me. "Everybody gets tested, one way or other," he said.

"Sure."

"We all liked Nicky, but he was a fuck-off. You can't have your life depending on a fuck-off."

"I reckon so."

"Sorry it had to happen the way it did. Must of made you feel bad."

Barry hadn't been there when I lost my cool. The tone, the eyes in the dark face were innocently sympathetic. But he could have heard about it by now and could be faking to draw me out.

"I was a mite shook up," I said. "But when you

come right down to it, I didn't really know him. Or any of you."

"You know me, Brother Thomas. And you know the other brothers and sisters. We your home, man. We all part of the same thing."

"How do you know I'm not like Nicky?"

"All it needs is Brother Persival saying you are part of it. That's all that matters. We all came up through the Church, but that don't mean everybody has to. You got family in the Church, that daughter, right?"

"Wherever she is."

"They looking for her. Don't worry."

"Is there any rule about taking a bath in the creek?"

"None at all. The best bath hole is upstream from the great big rocks, past the little trees. Take a towel off the line if there isn't one in your trailer."

It was a good solid yellow soap, and it worked well enough in ice water. I took my change of clothes with me and washed out the dirty ones, carried them back to the encampment, and hung them on the community line, along with my washed-out, wrung-out towel.

Then Chuck came and got me for lunch. With his drooping mustache, he looked like a Scandinavian travel advertisement. Haris had made some deerburgers, fried with onion. They sat me at the middle of the table, where I could get the full benefit of the love-buzzing, the hush whenever I spoke, the smiles and eye contact and shameless flattery. Yes, they all knew as soon as they saw me that I would be a wonderful addition to the group. Just wonderful. Just what they had been waiting for. Persival and Alvor sat alone at the other table, talking in low voices.

The conversation was slightly strained, and I guessed it was because they felt they should not talk about Nicky, but he was ever-present on the edge of memory. I made a few fruitless efforts to steer the conversation toward politics and violence, but they fielded them deftly and threw to another base.

After cleanup, a screen was set up and a projector wheeled out. I thought I was going to hear a tape by the celebrated Sister Elena Marie, but it was a creaky old black-and-white motion picture about The Long March, with a noisy sound track, a voice-over with a marked British accent, a lot of running, shooting, and gesticulating. They marched across China and up into the hills and caves, while my chin kept dropping onto my chest and I kept waking with a start. It ended with a loud blast of martial music which roused me enough to get up and say good night and go back to my trailer. I couldn't find the light switch and finally gave up and went to bed in the dark.

I was awakened by the click of the latch on the flimsy door of the trailer, a stealthy and barely audible squeak as it was opened. I wondered if one of the team had decided to correct Persival's decision to keep me alive. I moved in the bunk until I had my shoulders against the wall, until I was braced to move as quickly as I had to.

The generator was silent, the encampment dark. Just enough starlight came through the window above the bunk for me to make out a pale figure moving toward me. It stopped a couple of feet away, and I heard a silky whisper of fabric, caught a faint scent of female, and realized that Nena or Stella was paying me a visit. I guessed I had been asleep for an hour.

She picked up a corner of the blanket and came sliding into the bunk, shuddering with the cold, reaching to embrace me. I faked a great start of surprise.

"It's me, Brother Thomas," she whispered. "It's Stella."

So I was being gifted with the sallow blond lady with the inadequate jaw. "What's going on?"

"Well, whatever you want to go on. Okay?"

"Whose idea is this?"

"What difference would that make?"

"I'd like to know."

"You do a lot of talking, huh?"

I caught her questing hand by the wrist and took it away from me and said, "Is there anything wrong with wanting to know?"

"Look, are you okay? I mean, you make it with women?"

"I like to talk first."

"Jesus Christ!" she said. And then, "I'm sorry. That's blasphemy. But, you know, you are something else."

She turned onto her back, trying to separate herself from me totally, but the bunk was too narrow. Hip rested against hip, shoulder against shoulder.

"All it is," she said patiently, "you're new. Probably they don't want you being restless and wanting to sneak off or anything. So you get food and shelter and, once in a while, a piece of ass. What does it cost? Nothing but time, right?"

"You sound as if you did some hooking."

"I was into it. So?"

"Where was that?"

"So you're another one of those."

"Another what?"

"When I was a hooker, there was always a trick who wanted to know how I got into that line of work."

"Stella, settle down. Where are you going, anyway? Why the hostility? I can ask about you because I'm interested in you, can't I? Is there a house rule against that?"

She took in a deep breath and let it out slowly. "Well, okay. I'm sorry. When I came in here, I was really ready, you know? I don't feel that way very often. But what happens, you want to talk. So I'm losing the edge. It's fading on me. I think I got that ready on account of Nicky dying. Death does it to me in a funny way, I guess. When somebody you know is suddenly dead forever, then I want to get laid. I've heard lots of people are like that. Like in shelters when there's bombing going on. Maybe it goes back to instinct. Like in animals. If people are dying, it's time to make more people and keep the population up. But there was a couple of years there when I couldn't have come no matter what."

"What do you mean by that?"

"If you want talk instead of tail, I'll give you talk. I'm from an absolutely nowhere place. Opportunity, Montana."

"Little west of Butte? South of Anaconda? Flint Creek Range and the South Fork?"

"Hey, you heard of it!" She turned and settled herself more comfortably, fitting the nape of her neck to my arm, one hand resting on my chest.

"Been through there. When did you leave?"

"A long time ago. I don't know who's left there, if anybody."

"Run away?"

"Sort of. With a girl friend. We got in with some rough people in Miami. I got busted for possession, and when I got out, I couldn't find her. A cop put me on the streets, hustling. Then one day he beat me up bad because he thought I was holding out, and I met some people from the Church of the Apocrypha."

"In Miami?"

"You'll find the Church everywhere these days.

What I was thinking, I could *use* the Church. They'd take care of me and keep that freak cop away from me. I'd been beaten real bad. What I was then, I was a dumb, selfish, ignorant teenage hooker. What I needed most was some rest from cruising the streets and taking the marks back to that motel room. When I was rested up, I'd take off. But the people in the Church, they knew what I was thinking every minute. They never gave me a minute alone. They loved me. They believed I was precious and they made me think of myself as precious to them. I was a lazy little slut, and they cured me of that. My God, I never worked so hard and so long in my life. It made hooking seem like picnics. Dumb dreary food and not enough sleep ever. Fifteen hours at a stretch, selling stuff to strangers, walking the streets carrying candy and thread and junk, begging money, making quotas. My weight went down to minus nothing. A lot of my hair fell out. I had a scaly rash all the time. I forgot about sex. I stopped menstruating. My tits and my ass like to shrunk away to nothing. And when I was about to believe the life was going to kill me, suddenly I realized I was doing God's work, and that I wanted to drive myself even harder than they were driving me. And once I saw the Light and heard the Word, I started to get better. I ate tons of that sorry food they served at the dorm, and it tasted delicious. And I began to sell more stuff. I *made* people buy it. I turned in big scores every night and slept like a baby. I smiled and sang all the time. The Church had put my head back on straight. For the first time in my life I was *really* part of something. My life had meaning. I worked hard for the Church and for myself, and finally they picked me for a different kind of work."

"This kind? Guns and bombs?"

"It's God's work."

"You said you joined the Weather Underground, didn't you?"

"I didn't join them. It was sort of like cooperative, you know? They bought me a plane ticket out to Portland, and a fellow met me at the airport and drove me practically all day in an old car way down into empty country where they were. I thought I was in pretty good shape, you know? Talk about pooped! I used to get so tired I'd cry. But by three months, I could like run all day, you know? And I felt really alive. Then, when I could move right, they started all the other stuff. Weapons, marksmanship, cover and concealment, grenades, booby traps, reading a compass and maps, and all that. They taught me stuff I never heard of. You know, I could go into the average kitchen anywhere in the States, and in about twenty minutes I could build a bomb you wouldn't believe, just using what's already there."

"I forget where you said you went after that."

"First I went back to Miami, and they took me . . . someplace where I met Sister Elena Marie, and

177

it was the most wonderful thing that ever happened to me. She's fantastic. She knew all about me. She even seemed to know what I was thinking. She told me I was doing very well and I was one of the special ones planned by God for a special purpose. They got me a passport to Amsterdam and I went with a Brother who'd been there before and from there by car to Sofia, and he turned me over to some sort of official who took me out to the camp. It was a lot the same as Oregon, except different weapons and a lot of stuff I can't talk about. And, well, I got back to Miami, let me see, this is right after Christmas, and so it must have been seven months ago, and so I've been here six months. And maybe it will be six more before we . . . begin."

"Begin?"

"You know. We have to be given our assignments and we have to have a lot of time studying and working and planning so that it will all be automatic. Then we'll just, you know, go do them. It has to be all coordinated in order to work. We all have to be terribly, terribly careful."

"I saw you practicing something, you and Nena, and I think it was Haris and Ahman. Chuck was coaching and timing you."

"Oh, hey, you shouldn't have seen that! Please don't tell anybody, or somebody will get in trouble for not figuring out maybe you could see it. We didn't know what would happen with you, and we thought you would probably be killed. Maybe that's why somebody got careless. But there is always the very small chance you could get away, and if you could make somebody believe you when you told what you saw, then it might make big problems here."

"What were you doing? Your assignments?"

"Oh, no. That's just the Circle of Fire. It's all in the speed, getting ready. Then it's tricky how you set the weapons. You put them on full automatic but you have to learn to give just the quickest little touch. *Bzzzzt, bzzzzt, bzzzzt,* like not more than five or six shots each burst. You touch the trigger when the targets are thick enough in front of you. You keep it at belly level, because that's the way the most damage is done in a crowd."

Yes, indeed, I thought. Get the adults in the belly, the kids in the chest, and the littlies in the head bones.

"Will that be your assignment?"

"Oh, no. That would be a waste of people like us. They say there are people to do that who know how to do just that, and they're willing to do it. I think there's a special place where they train. They don't need as much physical training or training in a lot of different kinds of things. We were just doing it as a kind of a training exercise. That's all. So we *can* do it if we have to someday."

"It would be hard to do."

"I know. I know." Her tone was subdued and thoughtful.

I didn't know where to take it from there. I had to assume the trailer was bugged. Yet she would know if it were, and she wasn't sufficiently guarded. She wasn't hesitant in the way people are who know the tape is running.

"It's hard to see the point in doing it at all."

"Doing what?"

"Well, killing innocent people."

"Innocent of what, Brother? If you kill soldiers or police, it doesn't make enough difference. They signed up to take that risk. The people in this country are oppressed and they don't know it, and they don't give a damn. All the rest of the world is involved in a bitter struggle, and here the people are fat, happy, and dumb. The captive press and the television keep telling them they are the best people in the world in the best country in the world. The dirt and pain and sickness and poverty are all covered up. No person has a chance against the capitalist bureaucracy. We've learned that little attacks here and there are meaningless. Like fighting a pillow. They actually think they're free, the fools, even while they are supporting a regime that exports arms all over the world to the other oppressors. We have to make this fat dumb happy public sit up and take notice of the hidden tyranny that is oppressing them. How do we do that?"

Such a lot of it was by rote, repeated from

memory in a sentence structure alien to her usual patterns. "How *do* we do it, Sister?"

"We make the oppressors visible to the people by giving them reason to show how cruel and tough they can be. We force them to react. Like Chicago and Kent State, but much much more."

"By going out and killing people?"

"That isn't the purpose, Brother. To kill people. Our civilization has gotten too complicated. It's full of machines and plastics. Brother Persival says it is very sick, and like a sick person, it can't survive if a lot of other things happen to it."

"Such as?"

"Oh, we won't go after things that are really protected, like army places and shipyards and nuclear power plants and government buildings. That's dumb. You can bring everything tumbling down by going after things that would take years to fix. Big gas pipelines and oil pipelines. Bridges and tunnels and big computer places. Refineries and chemical plants and control towers. TV stations and newspaper pressrooms. Blow 'em up and burn 'em down. Targets of opportunity. Anyway, it's all being worked out. And then we'll know what our part of it is. I hope I don't get stuff to do that's too hard. I mean I want to be able to get it done. Then if I get away, okay, and if I don't, okay. But I'd hate to mess up. I hope I don't get a tunnel. I get really itchy going through tunnels. I think of all that water coming down on me."

"How do you do a tunnel?"

"Two people and two vehicles, right? The second one is an old truck. You've got a good big load of explosives, labeled something else. It takes a big blast. The lead car stops and you stop the truck and yank the wire that starts the three-minute timer. Then you run and get in the lead car and get out of there. It's the same for some kinds of bridges. I really don't want to do a tunnel. They make me so nervous I'll do something wrong."

She had turned onto her side, worked her head onto my shoulder. Her arm lay across my chest, her knees against the side of my thigh. She sighed and said, "I didn't have any interest in sex at all until I was in training overseas. Then it started to all come back. It's like that with most of the women who join. I mean the Church becomes the most important love life you have, and it wipes out everything else for a while. Then it's never as important again as it once was to you." She kissed the side of my throat and said, "Enough of all this talking already? You want to make it now?" She snugged the length of her body against me. This was a frightening little engine of destruction, all trained, primed, toughened, waiting only for someone to aim it at a target. Her breath had a faint scent of the deerburger onions. Her hair smelled clean, and her body had a slight coppery odor of perspiration. I remembered noticing at the table that her fingernails were chewed down to the quick.

Poor little assassin. She had gone out into the world with an empty head, and somebody had crammed a single frightful idea into it, dressed up with a lot of important-sounding rhetoric. She couldn't know the frightfulness of the idea because she had nothing by which to measure it. Fifteen to forty groups of from eight to fifteen? From a hundred and twenty to six hundred of them. So take the smallest number, cut it in half, and think about sixty people like this one, armed, mobilized, superbly equipped, and aimed at the pressure points of our culture.

I remembered one of Meyer's concepts about cultural resiliency. In the third world, the village of one thousand can provide itself with what it needs for survival. Smash the cities and half the villages, and the other half keep going. In our world, the village of one thousand has to import water, fuel, food, clothing, medicine, electric power, and entertainment. Smash the cities and all the villages die. And the city itself is frail. It has little nerve-center nodules. Water plant, power transmission lines, telephone switching facilities.

I was beginning to learn the purpose behind Brother Titus, and the reason for all the extraordinary caution.

And if that extraordinary caution carried over to all things, and assuming the trailer was not bugged, then Stella would be asked to give a report about her lovemaking with Brother Thomas.

"Oh, all we did was talk. He asked a lot of questions and we talked, and then after all that, he didn't want to. He said he wasn't gay, but he just didn't feel like it."

She had begun to use her hooker skills, and I had begun to respond to her. After all, what the hell. She was skillful and knowing. To her I was a tumescence of a certain length and girth, differing hardly at all from the many hundreds of others. Emotions need not be involved. I would think only of sensation. It did not have to have anything to do with mind and memory. As I began to switch roles from submission to domination, I told myself I could not, in any circumstances, think about the face and body and love of Gretel Howard.

I sagged back beside Stella and she said, "Hey, what happens?"

"I'm sorry."

"Did something about me put you off, honey?"

"No. It wasn't anything like that."

"What then?"

"I don't know."

"This sure isn't turning out to be one of my better nights."

"I'm sorry."

"Look, I'm not sore. You know what I think it was? It was being conned into shooting Nicky like you did. Something like that, if you're not used to it, can really shake you up inside. And then me coming in here like this when you weren't expecting it. And after all, Brother, you are not some eighteen-year-old guy who can get it off before he's unzipped. These things happen. Don't worry about me. I lost it too. Too much talking."

"I'm sorry."

"Let's just talk. I kind of like talking to you. And maybe we can have a little nap, and after that maybe we'll both be okay again, you know? How about that?"

"All right."

"You sure I didn't spoil it for you somehow?"

"No. You're . . . an attractive woman."

"I'm not much. I've got a pretty good body, compared to most. But I've got this tough yellowy skin, and if you look close, one eye points out a little bit, the right one. And the receding jaw. You know, I was saving up for an operation, a fellow that puts some kind of bone from your hip or someplace back here by the corners of your jaw and that pushes it forward, and then they fix your bite. I saw before-and-after pictures. It would really make a big difference. But that's vanity, isn't it? I'll be twenty-six in two months. I used to think about marriage and babies. I think I'd be okay with babies. Better than they were with me, I know. My dad broke two fingers on my left hand once, grabbing me when he lost his temper. They say if you've been abused, you abuse your own. I can't believe that. I'd be okay with kids. But there's no point in even thinking about it now, is there? By this time

185

next year, I'll probably be dead. Like Nicky. He just went a little ahead of the rest of us."

"Are they supposed to be suicide missions?"

"Not really. Everybody is supposed to do their best to get away. And we'll be given a staging area to go to where we can be regrouped and re-equipped and given new assignments. But if a person keeps doing it, how many times can you get away?"

"Everything will be in a state of confusion."

"You can believe it."

"But you know who is going to suffer the most, don't you?"

"Sure. The bottom layer of society. The poor and the minorities and the old ones. They won't have the money to take care of themselves when the food and the water and the medicines run out. They won't be able to run. That's when they'll rise up against the state. Then there'll be some kind of burning and killing. That's when the whole thing goes to hell for sure."

"And who takes charge after that's all over?"

"The Church has plans, Brother. Big plans. You just wait. Big plans." Her voice trailed away and her breathing changed and deepened. A woman of her times. Ready to aim the Circle of Fire, belly high. Happy to be caressed, glad to make love. Good with babies, and no good with tunnels.

I had blundered into something extraordinary. A

cult that was a cover for a deadly activism. Supported by curious international cooperations. I wished I could talk to Meyer about it. I really had nothing to go on. I knew the temporary location of nine people and a cache of arms and explosives. One out of fifteen or forty of unknown size and location, of unknown target date. Meyer had said, many times, that we run a strange kind of country in the modern world. Customs and Immigration are in a sense token services. Any plausible-looking person can find many ways to come and go unimpeded. Anything that can be flown or floated can be brought in or taken out. We are a wide place in the road in the middle of the world, and they wander through, back and forth, marveling at the lack of restraints. It is, Meyer pointed out, a paradox. The openness which endangers our system is the product of the policy which says that to close our borders and enforce all our rules and back them up with guns would change the system just as completely as any alien force.

I hoped there were enough tough young men like Max and Jake. I hoped somebody had this whole operation taped and wired. I hoped there were long lenses peering through the pine forests, and a lot of career people making little marks on important maps.

Gray daylight was seeping into the trailer when I awakened. She was standing beside the bunk, pulling the long T-shirt down over her head, smoothing it to the contours of her hips with the backs of her hands.

She smiled and leaned and kissed me lightly. "Hey, we slept too long. I got to go on kitchen duty. We'll try it another time?"

"Sure."

"Listen, don't worry about me saying anything, okay? I mean about you couldn't get it up. You're worried about a lot of things. All this is new to you, right? And your daughter missing and all. Anybody asks me, I'll say we like to screwed ourselves to death."

"Thanks, Sister."

"Don't you worry about a thing. Everything is going to be okay for you here. We'll all be looking out for you, Brother Thomas."

I heard the door close and she was gone. I rolled up in the two scratchy blankets and thought about Gretel in her agony, Gretel on fire. I knew how she would react if I could tell her she had been a victim of some kind of crazy political action cult, of people who wanted to remake the world by tearing it down and starting all over again. Cave people, trying to reinvent penicillin, Zippo lighters, and disco.

It has nothing to do with me, I told Gretel. I never think about stuff like this. It hurts my head. I think about the blue sea and tan ladies and straight gin with lots of ice. I think about how high out of the water a marlin might go, and how much of Meyer's chili I can eat, and how very good piano sounds in the nighttime. I think about swimming until I hurt, running until I wheeze, driving good cars and good boats and good bargains. Sure, I do my little knightlike thing, restoring goodies to the people from whom they were improperly wrested, doing battle with the genuinely evil bastards who prey on the gullible, helpless, and innocent. I was going to keep on doing that from time to time, to support you and me, girl, in the style we like best, if you had consented. I know from nothing about terrorism, funny churches, and exotic murder weapons, like the one they killed you with.

But here I am. In a sense, I was hunting for you.

I have killed one of them in a strange way. And nearly made love to another. I am in it now. I am going to let them run me and see what happens. And I swear before whatever gods there be, including even the one these crazies bow down to, that if they give me the faintest whispery breath of a chance, I am going to blow them all away, every one, without mercy, without hesitation. If I saw a fire starting in a kindergarten, I would throw water on it.

One down and nine to go. This time, my dead love, I am not doing my knightly routine. I have shelved that as inappropriate for the occasion. The old tin-can knight had too many compunctions, scruples, whatevers. For this caper, I am the iceman. I have come here and brought the ice. It is a delivery service. One time only.

12

On Thursday, two days after Christmas, I had my first experience of listening to Sister Elena Marie. It was set up at midafternoon in a small cement-block building the same size as the one where I had been locked up.

Chairs and stools were brought in. The camp generator was cranked up. A Sony color set rested on a low table, with a videotape deck beside it. Blankets were hung to shut out the light from the two windows. There was a feeling of expectancy, a muted excitement. Alvor was the only one missing. Stella sat close beside me.

Persival, almost invisible in the dimness, said, "Let us pray. Our Father, we thank thee for the opportunities which are being given to us. We are humbly grateful to be given a chance to play a part in the great events which will reshape life in this world and the future of humanity. We pray that we will be worthy of your trust in us. Our strength, our resolve, our determination, will all flow from your endless power. Since last we met in this room, one of us has been taken to your kingdom. Forgive our Brother Nicholas for his transgressions, his failure to comprehend the stern disciplines required of your children. There is a new one among us, a Brother Thomas, who came to us in search of his daughter and who has been thinking of remaining with us, adopting our vows, our ways, and our great mission. He is still uncertain, Lord. He is still confused. We are healing his lonely heart. Please give him the understanding of us and our ways so that he may join with us in our resolve, that he may become willing to sacrifice himself if necessary, in your bidding. We are thankful to you for providing this chance to hear, now, our beloved Sister Elena Marie speak your words from her heart. We are together, Lord. We are all as one. We are all united together in your holy cause. Amen."

Chuck stepped forward and switched the set on, and when it warmed up, he turned on the Betamax with the tape ready to roll.

The head and shoulders of Sister Elena Marie filled the screen. She stood silently, making a strong eye contact with everyone who looked into that screen. She was in color, long warm chestnut hair with golden lights in it. It hung to her shoulders. Oval face, clear features, a look of breeding and composure. Minimal makeup. Eyes of a most unusual shade of blue, almost a lavender blue. Wide eyes, set far apart. Flawless complexion, but with the small signs of age. I guessed her at about thirty-six to thirty-eight. Broad mouth with both lips equally heavy.

There was background music, soft music, an organ doodling with simple chords, as when the crowd has assembled, awaiting a wedding. Or a funeral service.

The music trailed off. She took a step closer to the camera. Just the face filled the screen. It was not a professional production. The camera was evidently stationary. No detail of the shadowy background was visible.

"Brothers and Sisters of the great Church of the Apocrypha," she said. Contralto resonance. Lovely diction. She could have played the Mrs. Miniver part with distinction. "I am looking into your eyes, your special individual eyes, the windows of your soul. I am looking through your eyes, into your heart, into your deepest thoughts. There is nothing you can possibly think that would surprise or dismay me, or make me love you the less. I know of all the dark and evil places that exist in every man and woman, the places we hide from each other and even from ourselves. It is only by joining together we can overwhelm the darkness within and the darkness without."

She paused for several seconds, widening her lovely eyes slightly. I did have the impression that she was looking further inside me than I wanted her to.

"Each one of you has a special place in my heart. I do not love you as a group. One cannot love people en masse, in the abstract. I love you for yourself, for the struggles you have made in the name of goodness and justice and freedom in the world, and for the sacrifices you will make in the future. Though I appear to be talking to everyone in this room, I am talking to you alone. To you!"

Pause. Slow bat of long eyelashes and a half smile, personal and almost sensuous.

"We *are* alone, you know. You and I. Everyone. But we have found something which eases the pain of the essential loneliness of every human. We are together in our purpose. We are all part of one another, forever. In all the endless dying and rebirthing, in all the aeons of time over which we will return here, again and again, we will know and recognize one another, just as we have during this time on earth, and if in some future time it is necessary for all of us to come together again, and save the world and humanity from an epoch of commercial slavery, cruelty, and shameful exploitation, then we will do so, we of the Apocrypha!"

Her voice had risen and strengthened. Though I

couldn't decide what she was saying, I found it very stirring. It was flattering somehow to be part of a purpose so great that it overlapped all the thousands of years ahead.

She moved back just a little, then gave a smile of apology. "Now I must ask you once again for patience. We must proceed with the greatest caution or lose the element of surprise on which we must depend. Our many friends in other nations are helping us, just as they promised. You know that perhaps even better than I. Some small arrangements have been delayed for the sake of greater safety. The transport of incoming supplies is a delicate problem, and it is being solved every day. And every day more of us are being trained. Warehousing, transport, and supply. Everyone is working very very hard on these problems. There is always the danger of penetration of security. Be ever alert. Our technical staff is identifying more pressure points as time goes by. Think of it this way. The longer we have to wait, the greater the blow we can strike. Continue with your training. You are the soldiers of the Lord! You will put him back upon his throne on earth, and you will live all of your days in peace and love and freedom forever."

She closed her eyes, and the lights that shone upon her face and hair were slowly, slowly dimmed until the screen was dark. The Betamax made a clacking sound, and Chuck leaped to turn it off, then sat again.

Persival said, "Sister Nena, please give the closing prayer."

She was behind me. I heard her stand. "Dear Lord, we thank thee for the privilege of hearing Sister Elena Marie speak your words with her sweet lips. Grant us the patience to endure the waiting, and the skill and the bravery to overcome all odds when at last we march in thy service. Amen."

She rattled it off so quickly I knew it was rote, and I suspected that I was probably the only one in the room who could not say the usual closing prayer.

Someone pulled the blankets away from the windows, and we were suddenly all squinting in the bright afternoon light. I looked at the television set and the tape deck. They were standard consumer items. But the way they were used was very professional. Very effective. These people seemed exalted by what they had heard. They beamed at each other and touched each other in ways of affection. I did an appropriate amount of beaming and touching. They were holding Sister Elena Marie in their hearts. She had come across to each one of us as an individual. She spoke to aloneness, in warmth and comfort.

I asked Brother Chuck if there were any old tapes I could hear.

"We don't keep any around. We'll show this one

again tonight, and everybody will want to hear it again. Then I erase it and put it back in the mailer and send it on back. They dupe the ones for the camps from a master they make at headquarters."

He looked at me with a telltale intentness. It was the game of which hand holds the marble. I got instantaneous help from my actress friend of long ago. Tom McGraw would ask.

"Where *is* headquarters anyway?"

"Classified," he said, smiling, whacking me on the arm.

"When do we get the next one?"

"There's no schedule. When she has something to say to us, she makes a tape, and they dupe it and send it out. They cost a lot, those tapes, so they get sent back blank to be reduped."

I wandered on out. I filed an item in the back of my mind. Somewhere in America, Betamax tapes were being sent in to a central place. If they were saving money on tape, they wouldn't be wasting it using couriers. If it were my problem, I'd use the mails. And I would have a permanent filler on the first fifteen minutes of each tape. They would be plainly labeled as church property, and they would have some old duck in a backward collar reading a dissertation on the philosophical impact of Martin Luther on political thought in middle Europe. And then the Sister. I would have them sent to a mail drop for courier pickup and delivery to home base. So if I happened to find the mailing address, it would probably give me no help at all.

I sat through it again that evening, and the impact of her was intensified, if anything. She did not fade. She just seemed to get stronger. And it was difficult to shake the illusion that she was looking directly at me. I could not estimate how big a woman she was. There was nothing to compare her to. She was in perfect proportion and could have been three feet tall or seven and a half. Dark-blue velvety dress with lace at the throat. No jewelry.

After it was over, Persival got me aside and said, "I want you working out with the group tomorrow. Any objection?"

"Me? No. No objection. Only, what is being done to locate where my little girl is?"

"They're trying to find her, and when they do, they'll let me know immediately. Report to Brother Chuck at eight sharp. Field exercises."

"Wearing what?"

"Ask him now."

Chuck told me we weren't leaving the land the Church owned, one full section of land, mostly up and down and sideways, so we'd wear fatigues, a light pack, and an ammo belt, and carry a weapon. He and Ahman took me over to supply, after Chuck got the key. The biggest fatigues were a little high in the ankle and short at the wrist. I explained my shoe problem, and they found a pair of size twelve sneakers and some thick nylon-and-wool socks. Ahman threw me the weapon, harder than he had to. The light was bad, just the single bulb going inside the warehouse door, and I didn't grab it close enough to the balance point, so the muzzle end tapped me over the ear, drawing a drop of blood.

"Watch it," I told him.

"Watch out for yourself, Brother," he said.

"What is this thing anyway?"

"It's an Uzi," Chuck said. "Made in Israel."

"Very small and light. Good weapon?"

Ahman shrugged and said, "You won't be firing it. All you do is carry it. You'll be glad it's light before the day is over. Some friends picked up a couple of truckloads of these in Lebanon. So we've got some. Makes for nice confusion. Remember what Arafat said after Camp David? He said there hadn't been any terrorism in the United States, and now they had proved themselves ready for some. For a lot, baby. A big lot. So when they bring down some of the brothers and sisters with Israeli weapons, they'll wonder what the hell, won't they?"

I carried my issue gear back to T-6. The sneakers felt right with two pairs of the socks. I found the right hole for the belt, filled the canteen, and positioned it at a better place on the belt. Chuck had told me I would be carrying twenty pounds of rock in the backpack, so I made careful adjustment of the straps, bringing the padding to the exact place where the straps hit the tops of my shoulders. Then

I inspected the Uzi under the light. It hadn't been built for pretty. It was an ugly, simple, straightforward little weapon. The empty clip snapped into place easily. It had a good balance, and a simple three-way control for safety, single fire, and full automatic. It looked designed for quantity production. I couldn't give it full approval until I had a chance, if ever, to fire it. Then I would learn the cycle of fire and whether it would ride up at full automatic, or whether the gases were diverted just right to make it easy to hold on target. It hung well over the shoulder on its fat little sling and came off the shoulder fast, with your hands falling into the right position. I had heard that since I had been around this kind of hardware they had upped the cycle of fire, upped the muzzle velocity to practically double, and reduced the weight of the projectile. A man could carry a lot more rounds into a firefight, do just as much damage with each hit, and hit oftener.

I was up early and observed the usual routine of the others—that wherever I strolled, somebody was keeping an eye on me. Brother Thomas was an unknown quantity.

When I had been wakeful in the night, I had realized that my assumption that they would mail the tapes had to be wrong. This outfit preferred to take no chances at all. It had to be a hand-delivery system, and so it would do no good at all to try to find a return address.

When I went back to sleep I dreamed of Sister Elena Marie, smiling at me, talking to me. It was very important that I understand what she was saying, but I could only catch a word or phrase here and there, and they were in a foreign language I could not even identify. She was telling me how to get around behind the screen, back to where she was, and she was becoming angry because I couldn't understand what she was telling me. If I could get on the same side of the screen as Sister Elena Marie, then Gretel would be spared. When I yelled at her in rage, it woke me up again.

I ate little because I had a good idea of what they were going to try to do to me. I guessed they could probably run me into the ground. But out of pride I wanted to make them have to stretch to do it.

They had six hundred and forty very rugged acres. It was a bright chilly day, at first. Chuck ran the group with whistle signals. I had to be briefed on those. Most of it was standard operating procedure for patrols. Infiltration, cover and conceal-ment, giving covering fire, without ammo. It involved a lot of running. I had a fifteen-year disad-vantage with most of them, and I was carrying eighty more pounds uphill than were the two girls. But they wasted energy in random movements. I husbanded every ounce, made no unnecessary step.

I was sweating heavily by late morning, and they all looked dry. They were conditioned.

There were special little moments of humiliation. Once when we had crossed a swollen creek and were going up an abrupt rocky slope on the other side, I got so winded near the top that I was grabbing small trees to yank myself along. As I was doing that, Stella went by me, running uphill on tiptoe, deft as a goat, and turned to give me a smile and a quick wink before leaving me behind, looking uphill at the bounding flex of those hips under the tough denim.

At another time, when I was breathing with my mouth open, gulping air hungrily, I sucked in a large California beetlebug, coughed him out violently, and couldn't stop coughing. But I was damned if I was going to say uncle. I was ready to drop first and be carried in. And I was also ready to cheat. I had weeded my twenty pounds of rock down to about three pounds. It helped.

When I was down to counting the minutes before I would probably pitch forward onto my face, I was saved by misadventure. Sister Nena took a good fast run to clear a creek, jumped well, and landed on a stone that turned as her foot struck it. She fell heavily on gravel, equipment clanking, and moaned as she reached for her right ankle. Her olive complexion was a yellow-white, her eyes squeezed by pain. I was first to reach her, and carefully unlaced the sodden sneaker and eased it off, then peeled the sock down and off her foot.

Chuck knelt beside me, and the others stood around looking down at her. "Busted?" he asked.

I told her to hold on tight, and I slowly manipulated the ankle joint. She sucked air. I made her work it herself. I knew from wide experience it wasn't bad.

"Just a little sprain, I think, but you shouldn't walk on it right away."

Chuck looked around at the slope of the land, the direction of distant peaks. "About a half mile back," he said.

Barry was wearing a macho silk scarf, off-white. Chuck wrapped the ankle tightly and tied it in place. I said I could carry her back. She said she could hobble and hop. She said it was her own damn clumsiness. Barry said he'd carry her. I said he could take over when I got tired. I didn't tell him I was already so tired I wondered if I could make a half mile by myself. Suddenly the sun was covered and the rain began to fall again. Chuck took my pack, hefted it, looked at me with a raised eyebrow, and dumped out the remaining rocks. Two of them. Apple-size. Barry took the weapon. Nena stood up on one foot, with Stella helping her balance. I bent and put my shoulder in her middle and had her lean forward as I stood up with her, my right arm wrapped around her legs just above her knees. She was smallish but solid. The rain refreshed me. It cooled me off. I made pretty good time. A few times I lost my footing on the uneven ground, and when I caught myself it would drive my shoulder into her middle, making her gasp. And each time I apologized, and each time she told me not to bother. Stella walked behind me, telling Nena how soon she would be up and around, which I knew was true. Barry offered twice to take over, but I said I was fine. I made it back in with her and, at Chuck's direction, took her to the trailer she shared with Stella. It was larger and older than mine. I bent over and knelt and perched her on the edge of her bunk, and she thanked me with an unanticipated shyness.

After the noon meal they went out again in the rain, but I was excused.

"We're doing some target work," Chuck explained. "We do it in bad weather when sound doesn't carry well and there's less chance of hikers around the perimeter."

"I could use some brushup on that."

"You're not cleared for live ammo, Brother."

"Brother Persival is the one who'd clear me?"

"When you're ready."

"What kind of weapon is that?"

He showed it to me but didn't let me handle it. "Pretty good. Better than it looks. It's Russian. Kalashnikov Assault Rifle. It's got a good reach, and it's fast and accurate enough. Of course, for real long-range accuracy, we've got better stuff. Scopes and all. Haris is the best one here at that game. He can hit a pie plate at a thousand meters on a still day."

"Good for Brother Haris."

"Is that being sarcastic or something, Brother?"

"No. I mean it's good shooting."

"Yes, it is." Off he trotted, tootling his whistle.

The camp seemed empty. I knew that Nena was in her quarters. I wandered around, wondering who was watching me. Somebody had to be on the gate. Alvor the silent one, if they hadn't rotated the duty. Persival had to be somewhere.

I thought it out during my aimless stroll in the misty rain. I had not passed any test. I had not proved anything to anybody. So somebody wanted to know how badly I wanted to take off. Would I go down the road or start out cross-country? What would Tom McGraw do? They had all Tom's money, and they were trying to locate his girl. So why not use up a piece of the rainy afternoon calling on the pretty little woman he had carried back to camp? Ask her how she was doing.

I rapped on the door and she called, "Come in?"

"How you doing?"

"Okay, I guess. I was so damn mad at myself. Sister Nena, the gazelle. See how she floats through the air." She was on the bunk. She had been reading.

"What's the book?"

She closed it and handed it to me. Worn binding,

dog-eared pages. *The Loving Heart* by Sister Elena Marie. "Hasn't anyone given it to you yet?"

"First I ever heard of it."

"You should read it. You should have your own copy. I guess somebody just forgot. It's wonderful. She's a great woman, truly great. I miss seeing her. I used to see her when I was in the regular camps. She used to visit. She still does that sometimes, I think."

"How long ago was that?"

"Five years. More than five. Nearly six."

"Back when you were twelve years old?"

She laughed. "Hardly. I'm twenty-eight."

"You don't look it. Nobody would guess. Were you at more than one of the regular camps?"

"Oh, sure. You get moved around. They don't want you to sink roots anywhere except in the Church. And a lot of us get moved because family has come to try to take us home. When we're already home in the best sense of the word. My mother spent a lot of time and money trying to find me and take me away. But that was a long time ago."

"Where is she now?"

"I wouldn't have the faintest clue, Brother. She is nothing to me. I have no interest in her."

"She's your mother, like I'm Kathy's father."

"That's a biological happenstance, Brother Thomas. I don't think we'll discuss that further. You have no right of approval or disapproval over anything I do or think or am."

"I'm just trying to understand is all."

"Don't try. Just accept. You're not open enough, Brother. You are closed up tight. Sister Elena Marie says there are answers which have to come before the questions."

"Makes no sense to me."

She looked at me with exasperation. "Will you try something with me? Will you let me try to show you something? Will you *really* try to cooperate, by that I mean letting things happen that try to happen?"

"Sure. Try what?"

"Can you sit there, on the floor, and cross your legs Buddha style?"

I sat and managed it, with a certain amount of creaking, saying, "Untangling myself will be something else again."

She smiled and settled down in front of me, not wincing at all as she moved her taped ankle into position, so close that our knees touched. "We take each other's hands like this, so that you are feeling the pulse here, in my left wrist, and I am feeling your pulse in your left wrist. Let the hands and forearms rest like this. Yes, so there's no strain. After a little while, if we are doing it right, our pulse rates will become identical, and quite slow. Like sixty beats per minute. Now you look into my eyes, not in any sharp focus because then you look at one eye or the other. Kind of unfocus a little, so you see them both. Unfocus as if you were looking beyond me. You can feel my pulse? Good. Now what you have to do is take long slow breaths. On each inhalation you say three words very slowly and distinctly inside your head. *We are one*. And you say it silently and in the same rhythm as you exhale. I'll match my breathing to yours, and then it should stay matched without my thinking about it. You say the words until they are meaningless, just sounds, like a mantra. What you have to do is concentrate on looking into my eyes and trying to hear the silent words I am saying. Try to hear my words inside your head and I try to hear yours inside mine. Stay aware of the pulse and the slow breathing. Keep your back straight and your eyes just a little unfocused. And try to kind of . . . *give* yourself to it, and let it happen. Start now. No, wait. I forgot. Don't let any outside thoughts come into your head. If you start to think of anything beside pulse, breathing, looking, listening, and the words, it sets you back. Okay. Go."

So I felt like an idiot. Sitting on the floor of an old trailer, doing some kind of mantra thing with a flaky female terrorist. But I did as directed. When Meyer was into hypnosis, he had me doing some odd things. I was difficult at first, until I realized that it wouldn't hurt me to try to cooperate. Then he could manage it. It delighted him. Going under seemed to make a little roaring sound in my head, reminiscent of the first few seconds before one passes out. I did as I was told, looking into Nena's dark wide eyes, and soon the little roaring sound started, taking me into a different level of consciousness. *We are one.* Quite suddenly I could hear her voice inside my head instead of my own. And I could no longer see the rest of her face with my peripheral vision, only her eyes. The breathing seemed to be becoming much slower. Her pulse was a very slow steady throb against my finger pad. It was all sensation, without thought. Going on and on and on.

I was aware that she had ended it. Her hands were gone from mine. Contact broken. It was like coming slowly up from the bottom of a deep clear pool, seeing the sunlight on the surface above. I gave myself a slow shake, like an old wet dog, and looked at her.

She was flushed, and looking at me oddly.

"What's the matter?" I asked her. "Worked pretty good."

"I know. Better than with most people when it's the first time. I didn't expect that. Knowing your background. Only the most sensitive and imaginative and intelligent people go into *semuanja baik* so quick."

"*Semu*-what?"

"It's an Indonesian phrase. It means everything is all right. Don't worry. Be reassured. Sister Elena

John D. MacDonald

Marie says it is synergy. One person plus one person equals more than two persons."

"Were you telling me I'm some kind of dummy?"

"No. It's just very strange you should get so deeply into it the very first time. It was . . . very stirring. And it makes a person feel very sexy."

"I noticed." She was still frowning at me. I felt certain she would report this unexpected facility to Persival and it would rekindle his doubts. I said, quickly, "I used to have this partner I'd go netting with. I used to get these headaches all the time. He said he could hypnotize me out of them, and he tried and tried and tried, and when he was about to give up, I finally went under. It helped a lot. So when you started this *semu*-something, it felt like it did when he was putting me under, so I let myself go."

She stopped frowning and gave a brisk little nod. "Of course. That would be it, wouldn't it? We use it to reinforce the joining together. When people begin to have doubts, when they begin to think they're not strong enough for what the Church demands, then they can do *semuanja baik* and be strengthened and refreshed. When I listen to Sister Elena Marie on the tape, I get sort of the same feeling. Not as intense, but it's there. That farawayness. Brother Persival says it's that quality that made her such a success when she was an evangelist. When she used to broadcast, with a choir of two hundred voices, from the Tabernacle in Biloxi. That was before she founded the Church of the Apocrypha, before she had taken the name Sister Elena Marie."

"What did her name used to be?"

"I wouldn't tell you except she was so well known a lot of people know it. She was Bobbie Jo Annison. She started preaching the gospel when she was sixteen. They got up to over a hundred and fifty stations toward the end, and she took in millions of dollars for good works. But she decided it was not the true faith, and there were too many advisers trying to run things, and the government was after her for taxes and all. And she decided that it was vanity that had taken over for piety, being on the air so much. So she quit and she founded our Church. Maybe it was about nine years ago, or ten. There used to be things in the magazines. Whatever happened to Bobbie Jo Annison? I expect you heard the name before."

"It sounds kind of familiar, but I was never much for turning on television for anything at all."

"She is the greatest woman who ever lived."

"You mean that?"

"I would die for her. I probably will die for her, and be reborn into my own identity in the next incarnation. That's the reward for dying for the Church. Sometimes, after I have prayed a long time, and very hard, suddenly I can hear her voice inside my head saying my words in her voice to the

Lord. Sister Stella can make that happen too. It's wonderful when it happens." Her face glowed.

"Speaking of Stella, maybe you can tell me the ground rules around here. I don't want to get into trouble."

"Because she came to your bed? No, there is no objection. It could have been suggested to her. I didn't ask and she didn't tell me. If the two of you slept only with each other, that would be bad."

"Is that rule in Sister Elena Marie's book?"

"Not in this book. In another of her books there is a chapter about sharing. She says that making love should be a simple function, and not be given too much importance in this era. She says that when we were all alive in earlier centuries, it was different. We were all faithful to just one person, and it was good and natural and right. And when we come back to earth again, in future centuries, it will probably be like that again. But now, in this world, if we begin to think too much of some other person, it will make us weak in our duty as soldiers in the Army of the Lord. We might forget our own mission in trying to save another person from hurt."

"Is this sharing okay in the other camps that aren't special? Like when my little girl was here?"

"Oh, no. You have to be celibate your first few years in the Church. You must give up everything for the Church. But we in special training have proved we will not be weakened by sexual pleasure, and if we wish it, it is permitted."

"As long as you spread it around."

"Is that some kind of a dirty joke to you?"

"I didn't know any other way to say it, Nena."

"You must call me Sister Nena, nothing else."

"How did you come to get selected for this training?"

"Everyone in the Church is watched. Actually they are testing all of us all the time, keeping track of the ones with the strongest faith and the strongest, quickest bodies. When they told me I had been selected for special training, I didn't even know what kind of training it would be. Now I know, and I'll do whatever they ask of me."

"Like blow up some kindergartens?"

"You really don't understand, do you? The most bloody, savage, awful acts that seem the most pointless, they're the ones that are most productive. They revolt and shock everyone, and that puts terrible pressure on the central government and local governments to crack down on *all* the people who are nonconformist in any way. When that happens, the resentment makes rebels out of the conformists too, and pretty soon the whole structure crumbles."

"And you can do these terrible things, Sister Nena?"

"I might be asked to do things that will make me feel sort of sick to my stomach. But I'll be proud of the chance to do them. I'm exalted to think I'll be part of something that's going to change the world. I'm proud of finally finding something in my life that makes sense, Brother Thomas. Has your life *really* made sense to you?"

"Sense? I don't know. I've had a few laughs. I've had some real good days. And some black black ones. Who says things have to make sense?"

"We *want* it to. Every one of us. We don't understand it, and Sister Elena Marie sorts it all out for us."

"Well, I wish I could go see the lady and let her explain it all to me."

"You saw the tape. Didn't that help?"

"I guess so. A little bit."

"Brother Thomas, we are all getting very fond of you, you know. We are enjoying having you with us. Please don't have doubts. Just don't think about it. Be open. And when the time comes, Brother Persival will have a mission for you, and you will want to perform it properly and please us all."

"Is that a first name or a last name? Persival."

"I really don't know. One of the rules of the Church is that everyone has just one name. And you can pick any part of your first name or last name, or you can make up a name, and then it is yours forever."

"Don't you get a lot of duplications?"

"Of course. What difference does that make? We don't pay taxes and we're not on social security and there is no payroll."

"Then it could be tough locating my little girl Kathy."

"In all the regular camps there must be hundreds of Kathys. People are supposed to forget their last names. So even if they paged her in all the regular camps, she might not answer."

"The boss lady has two names."

"Please don't call her that! She is the only person who is allowed to have two names. The only one in the whole Church."

I had untangled myself, and the feeling was coming back into my legs. She was back on the bed. By the way she moved I could see she no longer had an ankle problem.

"Well, take care of yourself, Sister Nena."

She smiled at me. "Sure. Sister Stella is very fond of you, did you know that?"

"I thought we were all very fond of each other. Isn't that the house rule?"

She pursed her lips as she stared at me. "Sometimes when you sound sarcastic you are like another person."

"In what way?"

"I don't really know."

I changed the subject. "Better stay off that ankle as much as you can."

"It's okay now. But thanks for carrying me."

I stepped down out of the trailer and closed the tin door. The misty rain had stopped. I did not see anyone around. I took a bath in the creek and changed to my other set of clothes and washed out the coveralls.

As I scrubbed away, I thought about my very few options. I could stay here and keep my head down and try to get a line on where their headquarters might be located, then try to sneak away somehow and report to that memorized phone number. I could plan and carry out some kind of group ambush, kill every one of them, and then hunt through all their stuff for clues about the rest of the organization. But even if I could see myself executing all these crazies, little girls and all, my ability to do it was questionable. They were trim and tough and wary. Splendid reflexes. I could hang around until my mission, and then defect once I was at sea on the boat I was going to have to buy. By that time things would be popping all over the country, apparently. Sniping, fires, explosions, massacres, and God knows what all.

And once again I saw Gretel's face, the way the fever had wasted her, saw her chest pumping as the machine breathed for her, saw the laugh-lines around her dying eyes.

And I thought then of a provisional plan. Nicky was dead. Maybe they would find out I wasn't what I had pretended to be. If so, the odds might be improved between now and then. Nine to one read better than ten to one . . . a little better. Keep the eyes open. Improvise.

I stood up quickly, turning as I rose, and saw a

216

flicker of movement beyond a big tree a hundred feet away. Suspicion confirmed. Keep an eye on Brother Thomas, but without giving yourself away. And we'll see what he does.

Well, he just hung around and washed himself and some clothes. He spent an hour with Sister Nena. He doesn't seem to want to take off.

That night I got up from the table and went over to where Persival sat with Alvor. I said, "I don't see any good reason why you have to hang onto my money."

"People in the Church have no need of money."

"I'm not in the Church yet."

"Your money is safe."

"You give me a list of the regular camps where my Kathy might be, and I'll go check them out, and then I'll come back here whether I find her or not."

"Would you try to take her away from the camp?"

"No. I just want to see how she looks grown up, and tell her that her ma is dead. That's all. I want to make sure she's alive."

"We're trying to locate her for you."

"You keep telling me that."

"What need would you have for money here? It's safe. Now go back and sit down, Brother. You're doing fine here. Don't spoil it."

"Suppose I decided to leave anyway."

They looked up at me. Brother Alvor had eyes like dry pebbles. Brother Persival said, "Then we'll

John D. MacDonald

bury you beside Brother Nicholas and say a prayer over you. And make do without you."

I know the truth when I hear it. I went back to the other table. The others were finishing. They looked at me with curiosity, but asked no questions.

They resumed their conversation. Chuck was being the instructor again. Topic, thermite pencils. "Remember, they maintain a temperature of twelve hundred degrees Fahrenheit for ten minutes. They aren't like the older ones we had. Those were too complicated. You twist this end one full turn, and that breaks the seal so that the acid starts to eat through the barrier. It will take two hours to eat through, plus or minus ten minutes. Remember, the secret is saturation. A team of four can start at a designated point in the heart of a city, and each head out in a different direction like the spokes of a wheel, on foot. The cover story is the distribution of pamphlets. Each team member can carry and distribute two hundred pencils. You've read the list of preferred types of locations. You walk ten blocks out from the primary target area and then, a half hour later, walk the circumference of an imaginary wheel, building a circle of future fire around the heart of the city. In that way you can trap most of the fire-fighting organizations between the two fires, and also we're told that this dispersion is the most effective way of creating a fire storm."

He was still talking when I walked out.

13

On Saturday, Sunday, and Monday, the last three days of the year, I tried to find out everything I could about the area. I located everyone's quarters and realized there was room for twice as many. Haris told me there had been more travel trailers, and what was now the warehouse had been a bunkhouse, capable of accommodating a hundred and fifty.

The one time I had looked into the warehouse, I had seen, in the light of the small bulb near the door, towering stacks of crates and boxes. It seemed to be much more than these few people could use or carry.

On Monday I learned by accident of one deadly

item they were warehousing. It was obvious I had no chance to get in there. I happened upon Ahman out behind the small mess hall, where the grass grew tall and coarse. He was backing away, looking intently at the grass. I did not see what he was looking at for a few moments, and then I saw it, a cylinder about three feet high, three inches in circumference.

"Hard to see it?" he asked. "I've been trying different ways of painting it. The damn things came through all shiny. I striped this one green and brown, vertically. It seems to work the best. Kind of wavy lines, like the grass."

I walked toward it with him. "What is it?"

"It's a little rocket."

"What does it do?"

"It does what rockets do, Brother. It goes *whoosh-bam.*"

"Thanks a lot."

He hesitated, then said, "It's on a spike, see? You shove it into the ground at a little slant. You find a good place, a half mile from the end of a runway. Then you pull this top cap off and throw it away. Then you unscrew this little cap down here near the base. Then you push this little switch, and from then on you make no loud noises, Brother. It is an acoustic trigger. A loud noise, like a jet going over low, closes the circuit, and that ignites the propellant and it comes out fast. Little vanes snap open. It's a heat-finder. Little heat-sensitive guidance system. It will pick right up to a thousand meters a second, which is somewhere around two thousand miles an hour. It has a four-mile range and it'll hit the hottest thing it can find, which will be a jet engine, and it's got enough muscle to blow off a wing or a tail, whatever. They come six in a case, labeled kitchen equipment, and we've got ten cases. It's a low-risk operation. The best way is a telephone company truck. You always see them off on back roads, and you never think twice about it."

"Commercial airports?"

"We certainly couldn't get close enough to military ones even if we wanted to."

"Where are they made?"

"It doesn't say. The instructions come in six languages."

I hoped I did not look as shaken as I felt. If only one out of every six ignited and hit a target, it would be the worst airline disaster of all time. "Ladies and gentlemen, we are on our final approach to San Francisco International Airport. Please put out all cigarettes and make sure your seat belts are fastened and your tray tables are in an upright position. It has been our pleasure serving you, and we hope you will fly . . ." *bam*.

He picked it up gently and, holding it so as not to smear his paint job, carried it off toward the warehouse. I went back into the mess hall. It was my turn on the food detail. I stared at the supplies and couldn't decide what to have. I felt queasy.

I jumped a foot in the air when somebody slapped me on the behind. It was Stella, back from her morning wars, grinning, showing a lot of uneven teeth. And smelling faintly of cordite.

"Hey, you got bad nerves, Brother Tom."

"Looks that way."

"I should come on by tonight and relax you. But, come to think of it, we'll have to make it another time. I'm on the gate midnight to dawn. What's the matter with you? You act down. Is anything wrong?"

"No. Everything is just peachy. Help me figure out what to cook up."

"Get out of the way. Let me see what we've got. Boy, there isn't much. But there's two less for lunch, and Brother Persival and Brother Alvor will be back later on with fresh supplies."

"Who's down on the gate?"

"Brother Sammy, I think."

"Should somebody take something down to him?"

"He can eat after he's relieved."

"I don't even know who runs the duty roster."

"Brother Chuck, mostly. Unless Brother Persival wants something done different. Have you been studying your book?"

"*The Loving Heart?* It sure isn't easy reading."

"You can say that again. You know, there are parts I have to skip every time."

"What I was thinking, if I could read some of it

into a tape recorder, one of those little ones I saw, I could learn it faster."

"Oh, I can get you one of those. We've got two in our trailer. And lots of empty tape. Want it right now?"

"Why not?"

She gave me a warm look and a loving smile and went trotting off, leaving her pack, weapon, and belt in the corner of the kitchen area. I moved close enough to it to see that the Uzi clip was full up. They get used to having you around. Good old McGraw. He's getting plenty of exercise, enough food. We've got his money and we're supposed to be hunting for his daughter. Keep an eye on him, of course, but nobody is exactly worried about him.

I had tried to give myself another advantage too. During the field exercises I had tried to keep going when it called for endurance, but I had dogged it when it was something calling for quick. I had blundered around when the order was for silent approach. When we ran the improvised obstacle course, I arranged to finish almost last every time. In unarmed combat, I let the men drop me with a certain amount of fuss and trouble. I was rounding off into top shape, putting on a nice edge. As I clumsied along, I studied each of them to see their flaws. Barry was muscle-bound from too much body building. Haris was very quick but without adequate physical strength. Sammy was too wildly energetic. He didn't plant himself for leverage, and he tried to move in too many directions at once. Ahman was quick and strong and crafty, once he had made up his mind, but he was prone to fatal hesitations. Chuck was the best of them, without a weakness except perhaps a tendency to exhibit more grace than was required, to turn his best profile toward an imaginary camera, to leap a little higher, spin more quickly than the exercise required.

Stella came back with a little cardboard box, silver-colored and battered, and repaired with tape. The Olympus Pearlcorder and accessories were in a jumble inside the box, along with extra tapes and batteries.

"Everybody will have to use one when we get the assignments," she said.

"How?"

"You have to memorize every word of your assignment, and you have to be able to start anywhere, in the middle, toward the end, anywhere. So what you do is read it onto the tape, and then before you go to sleep and when you wake up, you play it and say it right along with yourself, over and over and over. It has to be so much second nature that you don't have to think about it when you go out on an operation. They're very, you know, complete. 'You will get off at the corner of Main and Central. You will walk quickly north on Main on the right-hand side of the street. When you get to the bus stop at the southeast corner of Main and

Pearl, you will wait there until precisely fourteen hundred hours. You will turn and enter the General National Bank Building, take the first available elevator, and ride up to the fifteenth floor. You will turn left when you exit the elevator, follow the corridor to the fire door at the end.' And so on. That was only part of a practice operation I did. There were two more pages of orders. By the time I started it, I never had to think of what to do next. I knew. I was like some kind of machine, you know?"

I took the recorder back to T-6 and left it on the bunk and came back and helped her with the meal. Since it was the last day of the year, Persival had canceled all afternoon exercises and given orders for solitary meditation and rest. I acquainted myself with my tape recorder. There was an attachment to screw onto the bottom of it which worked as a voice-actuating device. I tested the sensitivity. I put a tape in and read some of *The Loving Heart*.

> "Just as white reflects all colors and
> black absorbs all colors, the Lord both
> reflects and absorbs all the thoughts and
> desires which pass through our mind.
> When you know that your thoughts are
> turning negative, that you are losing faith
> in your own faith, you must become one
> with a trusted Brother or Sister who loves

you, and through that person renew and restore each other to the positive glory of the Church."

I listened to it come back, with little clicks where it had turned off by itself and come back on again at the sound of my voice, sometimes eliminating the first syllable after the pause.

It amused me to think of what Meyer would say about this mishmash. Though perfectly willing to pursue the philosophical concept to the furthest thicket of his mind, he has no patience with imprecision of thought, looseness of expression.

I read the tattered Pearlcorder manual again and pondered where to place the device. Persival and Alvor were the ones I wanted to tap. Alvor had a little square cement house of his own. It resembled him. Persival lived in the most elegant accommodation of all, a fat tan motor home with bulbous rounded corners and six soft but not flat tires. In the evenings he would confer with Chuck or Alvor or both of them in his motor home. It had obsolete Arizona plates and was not readily visible from the broad flat area of the stony plateau.

One side of one tape was good for thirty minutes. Planting the machine was no good if I had no way to retrieve it.

The quality of the light had changed. I opened my door. Snow was falling, big fat flakes, melting as they fell, coming down in ever greater quantity, dimming the sky. As I stood there I heard the van coming. It stopped near the warehouse, and I went out to see if I could help, shoving the recorder into my pocket. There were some small heavy wooden boxes in addition to the supplies they had gone after. Chuck appeared, and as he and Alvor carried the boxes into the warehouse, I was detailed to move the provisions to the kitchen. It took four trips, and when I went back to the van, Brother Persival was standing, grimacing with pain, beside one of the small boxes which had fallen into the snow.

"I shouldn't have tried to carry it," he said. "Would you take it to my quarters, please, Brother Thomas? I'll be along in a few moments."

It was very heavy for the size of it and contained, according to the label, some sort of electronic equipment. The motor home was locked. I rested the box on the step. Just to the left of the door there was a metal grid held in place by simple plastic thumbscrew devices, two of them. I guessed it was to vent heat from the back of the refrigerator. I took out the recorder, set the sensitivity, put it on Automatic Record, undid one thumbscrew, pulled the flimsy metal out a few inches, and shoved the recorder into the small space inside and closed the grid again. It had been an almost instinctive reaction. I did not know how or when I was going to retrieve the recorder. I did not know if it would do me any good. Maybe, if the refrigerator was running, I would merely get thirty minutes of compressor effects. If Stella wanted the recorder back, I would have to say I lost it in the snow or the creek, or somewhere.

Within moments I was wishing I had it back, but Brother Persival came along to open the door. He did not invite me in. He told me to reach in and set the box on the floor. He thanked me, and I went away. I went to a spot where I could see who might be going in and out of the motor home. First Alvor and then Chuck. Then Alvor came out and went to his own place. Chuck stayed inside until it was time to start fixing the evening meal. Celebration. Among the supplies was a batch of barbecued chickens, needing only to be heated up. And there were several half-gallon jugs of Gallo Hearty Burgundy, and ice cream packed in dry ice. End of the year. Hooray for the New Year. Hooray for terrorism, for death and fire and confusion. We were all smiles and fun as we ate. Even Ahman was pleasant to me. Persival and Alvor ate at the big table with the rest of us. The snow was staying on the ground.

With no better plan, I managed a wine drunk. I sang. I kissed the ladies. I was a figure of fun. McGraw, the funny fisherman. Dads, we call him. I whacked Alvor on the back. It was very like whacking the side of his little cement house. And it got just as much reaction.

Suddenly I stopped and stood, weaving back and

forth, a hand clapped across my mouth, eyes wide with consternation, cheeks bulging. I plunged to the door and went out into the snow, leaving them laughing.

I made sure I left erratic tracks, but the tracks took me right to the motor home. I had just fastened the thin metal grille back in place when Sammy yelled, "You! Hey! Get away from there! What are you doing?"

I wheeled around and stumbled toward him, arms wide. "Good ol' Brother Sammy. Never knew I was gonna have a Chinese brother."

He tried to elude me, but I embraced him and began a horrible retching cough that panicked him. He struggled free and I fell to my hands and knees and said, "Gotta go home. Help me, old buddy. Can't find old T-Six. Somebody moved it on me."

He helped me up, and I staggered a zigzag course along the direction in which he was leading me. I mumbled thanks and crawled into my trailer. Five minutes later, when I looked out, there was no one in sight. I undressed and got into the bunk under the blankets. The tape had been used up. I rewound it. I used the ivory ear button to listen to it.

It was very indistinct. I experimented with the volume controls, trying to clear it. The voices sounded too much alike. It was Alvor, Persival, and Chuck, talking about people I didn't know. And they were too far from the recorder.

Alvor left the conversation. I could more readily distinguish between Chuck's and Persival's voices.

They both were muffled, but Persival spoke in slower cadence. "—three more here . . . Ireland . . . woman thirty . . . late January . . ."

"—about another vehicle?"

"Later. Maybe at the same time."

Mumble ". . ."

"—tentative approval . . . liked the basic idea. Oil tankers too . . . longer delay . . . arrive tomorrow . . . description of McGraw . . . take a personal look . . . coming up from . . . go back with him . . . you in charge."

And that was all I could get out of the half hour. The rest was all fragmentary, blurred, distorted. I played those parts over and over, trying to get another word or two. Somebody was coming on New Year's Day to take a look at their Mr. McGraw. As a card-carrying pessimist, I could expect nothing good from that. With such a big, careful, patient, rich organization, they would have sent somebody to check out the expired Florida driver's license with my face thereon. Probably sent the license itself. Maybe their Mr. Toomey or Mr. Kline took a look at the license. I had been too tricky. Always keep things simple as possible.

It meant I would have to choose one of my sorry options sooner than I had expected. The most attractive one was to take off in the snowstorm while they thought me drunk. Get to a phone somehow.

Call the number memorized at the request of Max and Jake. Hope they would believe me. Hope they would move fast enough.

I dressed warm. Poncho on last. I moved to the door, and just as I got there, it opened and Stella came in out of the snow and ran right into me.

"Hey, where are *you* going?"

"Me? I'm going back to the party."

"That party's over." She grinned. "And now we've got our own private one. You know, there isn't supposed to be this much snow here this time of year, staying on the ground." She gave me a push. "Back to the sack, lover. I got taken off the gate detail, and Nena has some company, so I've got to stay. Here, let me help you get that off, Brother Tommy. Honey, are you too drunk to make it? We'll find out. Don't worry about it. I got lots of ways to help you. Sit down, sweetie. I'll get your shoes off. There. Don't you worry about a thing."

When I saw the first faint pallor of dawn at the window, I made my move. She was asleep on the inside, face to the wall. I had to believe she had been told to stay close to me until tomorrow's visitor could check me out. I got up as quietly as I could and began dressing. Suddenly she rolled over and sat up and said, "Hey? Where you going?"

I held my finger to my lips and shushed her.

"What's going on?" she whispered.

I leaned close as if to whisper in her ear. When she lifted her chin, I popped her on the corner of the jaw with a right that traveled about six inches. In my tension and apprehension, I had hit her harder than was necessary. It bounced her head off the wall behind her and she sprawled face down into the pillow, motionless. I ripped her heavy twill shirt into strips, tied her up securely, poked a wad of shirt material into her mouth, and used the last strip to hold it there, with the knot at the back of her neck.

It was a very still morning, the first day without wind since I had arrived. Welcome to the New Year. The temperature was up, the snow beginning to melt. It made for bad footing. I knew I couldn't risk going too fast. Too many chop blocks in the old days had stretched the knee tendons almost to the point of surgery. I could land on something under the snow that would shift or turn, and from then on I could be caught by a reasonably spry turtle.

My plan was to get down the road as fast as I could, cut off at the last bend, and come up behind the lean-to. I was fifteen yards from the beginning of the road when there was a yell behind me. I turned and saw Barry back near the kitchen building, alone and unarmed. So I began to move a lot faster, hoping for the best. I had made a slippery hundred yards down the hill when I heard three spaced shots behind me and a long screeching blast on Chuck's whistle. I knew that would alert whoever was at the gate, so that plan was shot.

I turned off the road at an angle to the right, hoping to make a wide half circle around the gate and come back onto the public road. I soon realized I wasn't going to give them much trouble. It was very rough country. I couldn't try to brush away my tracks. The snow was too soggy. I couldn't go as fast as they would. They had good knees. I couldn't wait for the damn snow to melt. The only thing I could possibly try would be to make a circle, intercept my own trail, and ambush them. With snowballs, perhaps. And they would realize that this was my only option and would be careful to take the elementary precaution of spacing themselves a hundred feet apart and searching the snow on either side for tracks.

While thinking, I was making as good time as I dared. And I studied the terrain, trying to evolve some kind of plan. There would be at least two, and they would probably be Barry and Chuck, and they would have those little Uzis. I slid down a steep bank into a tumbling brook and scrambled up the rocky ten-foot slope on the other side, picking up a rock a little bigger than a baseball and tucking it into the slit pocket of the poncho, where it proceeded to chunk me on the hip every third step. But it was better than a snowball.

I came to a second, smaller creek. It was shallow enough, so I went downstream, stumbling on the

stones, splashing water up to my knees. It dipped
downhill abruptly, spilling over the rocks in a mini-
waterfall. I had to sit down to negotiate the drop.
Around two curves I came upon a place where the
racing water had gouged a chunk out of the bank
and toppled a big pine across the brook. It had
happened many months ago. The pine had wedged
itself against two large living trees on the other
bank and rested at about a 20-degree angle, cross-
ing the brook fifteen feet above my head.

I stopped and studied it a few moments, then
hurried on down the creek and around two more
bends, climbing out on the right-hand bank, making no attempt to disguise my exit across the fresh
snow. In fact, I purposely went down to my knees
and left them a clear handprint to give them confidence. I made a circle back upstream, and when I
was away from the rushing water, I stopped and listened. I could hear distant shouts. Then I heard the
van and assumed it was going down past the gate,
to take up a position on the public road to cut me
off if I went that way.

As I neared the fallen tree, I tried to conceal my
footsteps as much as possible. I stepped close to the
base of trees. I took long slow stretching strides. I
crept out along the fat trunk of the fallen tree on
my hands and knees, trying to dislodge as little of
the snow as possible. The thick dead limbs started
at mid-creek, sticking out at right angles from the
trunk. I was able to settle myself against two of

them, my chest resting on one, my thighs on another, out of sight behind the trunk from anybody coming downstream. By lifting my head I could look upstream. I dislodged a little snow on the trunk so I would not have to lift my head any farther than necessary.

I changed position enough to find a limb I could hook my ankles over. It helped. The position was uncomfortable. I could expect that they, if there were two of them, would both come downstream. It was my logical escape direction. I hoped they would be well spread out. I hoped the one in the lead would not stop and turn around, once past the tree, look back for his friend, and glance upward.

It seemed certain they would come down the creek itself. The terrain was so difficult they would be endlessly slow if they tried to walk beside it, each taking a bank and staying opposite each other. I guessed the temperature had moved up into the high 40s. The woods dripped. Clots of heavy snow fell off the pine boughs. I rehearsed my drop, thinking out each move. There was no time to practice.

It was taking longer than I expected. Suddenly I heard the heavy splashing sound of somebody walking swiftly down the creek. He passed under me. Brother Chuck. He moved well, knees slightly bent, keeping his balance, holding the Uzi in his right hand by the trigger assembly, swinging it to point at one bank and then the other as he swiveled his gaze back and forth. I did not breathe until he was out of sight. I waited for the next one. I hoped there was a next one. Then I heard the screech of Chuck's whistle. Two long blasts, carrying well in the morning stillness, piercing the sounds of the brook, the sounds of dripping from the trees.

So either he would be off and running along my trail, or he would wait there to be sure his number two didn't miss it. I wished I had made it more difficult to see.

Along came the splashing, more rapid than before. I couldn't risk a look. I jacked my feet up onto the limb on which my thighs had rested. I braced myself with my left hand against the limb which had been under my chest. I held my comforting rock in my right hand. When I caught the first glimpse of Chuck's number two emerging from under my tree, I slid my feet off the limb and dropped. I had turned slightly to my right, hoping to land with my feet on the back of his shoulders and pitch him forward into the water. I landed behind him and slammed the rock squarely on top of his skull. I went down, floundering to get up, expecting him to be ready to cut me in half. When I came up gasping, he was face down in fifteen inches of black water, the current slowly turning his feet downstream. I saw the glint of metal and picked the weapon out of the icy water, wondering if it would fire. My right knee would barely support my weight. I shifted the weapon to my left hand, grabbed Barry by the tough clothing at the nape of his neck, and dragged him out of the brook and up the bank to the left.

I had no idea how fast Chuck would be in getting to my tree. I knew he would be thinking as he ran, and as soon as he saw where my trail was going, he would think ambush. When I climbed up on the high bank, he wasn't in sight. Not yet. I looked at Barry. He had an ugly jellied depression half the size of my rock in the crown of his head. But I had no time for Barry. I saw movement. Chuck was coming fast through the trees. Too fast for me to risk jumping up and trying to hobble to shelter. Barry was at the top of the bank, on his back. I sat him up and lay prone behind him. I held him in position with the fabric between his shoulder blades bunched in my left hand. I checked the Uzi. It seemed to be on full automatic. I shoved it forward, under Barry's right arm, and found I could line up the sights.

Chuck disappeared behind the uptilted root structure of the big tree, then came back into view, very tense, crouched, swinging the muzzle from side to side. He looked over and saw his partner sitting on the bank, head on his chest, soaking wet, and I knew his first impulse would be concern, but his second reaction would be to jump back into the cover he had just left. He was quicker than I expected. I caught him in mid-jump and apparently hit him quite high—as he began a back flip before disappearing. I scuttled to my rear and hid behind a tree. When I let go of Barry, the body pitched forward and slid down to the edge of the creek.

I counted up to a reasonable number twice, and then once more for good measure. I circled, went back and crossed the creek above the little waterfall, came around, and finally saw Chuck on his face in the melting snow, his weapon a yard away from his right hand, resting against a rotting stump, as naturally as if he had placed it there.

I moved close enough to have seen him breathing, had he been. I moved in and rolled him over. One high on the right shoulder, two high on the right chest. Probably not instantaneous. He had probably faded away while I was counting.

"The iceman," I said aloud, and the sound of my voice startled me. No need to lose your wits, McGee. No need to talk to yourself in the forest deep. It was a pleasure to be McGee again. McGraw had been a tiresome fellow. Dogged and unresponsive.

I searched them both. I switched weapons. I kept Barry's small pack, Chuck's ammo belt, grenades, intricate wristwatch, whistle cord and whistle, all the clips, both sets of keys, and their combined treasury of forty-two dollars. Though the dead seem to shrink in size, it is hard to get into their pockets. They seem to offer a stolid resistance to personal invasion.

I kept a close watch upstream while robbing my brothers. My knee was coming back. I had progressed from a hobble to a gimp, and from experience I could tell that if I kept moving, it would work itself out the rest of the way.

There was an assumption to be made. Somebody had probably been near enough to the area to hear the distinctive flat drumming of the Uzi in a wasteful burst of about ten. It would be reasonable for them to suppose that Brother Chuck and Brother Barry had come upon Brother Thomas and cut him down in the snow. Since they had been trained in exactly this sort of thing, pursuit and murder, it was not reasonable to suppose the murderee had turned the tables. And I had given them cause to feel a certain professional contempt for the abilities of Brother Thomas. So now they would be waiting for Brother Chuck and Brother Barry to come back out to the road and report. Persival, Alvor, Ahman, Haris, Sammy, Nena, and—if they had found her and untied her—Stella.

Assume somebody on the gate and one person way down the road in the van—or off in the van to pick somebody up. Four left on top of the hill. Five counting Stella. So go in the least likely direction. Back to camp. The hard way. Up the slopes, well away from the road.

By now there was such a confusion of tracks, I doubted they could be easily read. Also, in places where the snowfall on the ground had been light because of the trees, it was melted enough to show the brown carpet of needles.

After a time I came to familiar terrain—where we had been on the exercises, on the training missions. I stopped and listened for a long time and heard nothing. Then I heard five spaced shots well below and behind me, very probably from where I had left the bodies. Five was Brother Chuck's emergency signal on his whistle, taken, no doubt, from the marine emergency signal, five quick ones on the ship's horn.

Probably two down there, one at the gate, one in the van, three on top of the hill, counting Stella. One with, as Persival himself had pointed out, very bad wheels. Alvor, Persival, and perhaps Stella.

All of them were convinced of the absolute correctness of their training, their dedication, their mission. A true zealot can be a fearsome engine of destruction. I worked my way up the slope. The small shattered trees were off to my left. I stretched out and inched forward until I could see all the way down the length of the small plateau. It was seven or eight hundred feet long, three or four hundred wide, with the structures grouped at the far end.

14

As I watched, I heard a motor. It was the van, coming up the hill, approaching rapidly. The road came out onto the plateau a hundred feet to my right. It bounced up over the final ridge so quickly I could not tell if there was one person in it or two.

It rolled to a stop near Persival's motor home and, as Sammy or Ahman got out of it—I couldn't tell which one it was at that distance, close to six hundred feet—Persival and Alvor came out of the motor home. They stood and talked. I could guess that it was excited talk. The newcomer was waving his arms and pointing back the way he had come.

I had the general idea of using the keys to get into the big warehouse building and then making as much all-around hell as I could with whatever I might find there. But my chances of doing that would be improved if I could keep the locals indoors.

There didn't seem to be too much danger in loosing a single shot in their direction. I set my little machine to Single Fire, according to the logo by the small knob. I did not know how much accuracy I could expect. But it did seem a useful idea to make a serious attempt to wing one of them. Alvor struck me as being the most ominous of the three. I aimed as carefully as I could at a spot six inches over his head and squeezed the trigger. The one who was Ahman or Sammy, three feet to Alvor's right, bent over abruptly and fell to the ground. The other two ducked into the motor home. The figure on the ground struggled to get up, then hitched along like a broken bug until he was out of sight around Brother Persival's dwelling. Splendid shooting! Aim at one, hit another. The slug flew three feet low and three feet to the left. I had had no real expectation of knocking anybody down at that range. The flat little smacking sound of the shot had seemed inadequate and potentially ineffective.

How now? I didn't want to lose my luck. It goes like that, like a giant crap table. One day in a firefight, you never see anybody. You keep falling down, jamming the weapon, drawing fire, and if you do see people, you're convinced you couldn't hit within fifteen feet of them. And a week later, fifty miles away, everything works. The grenade takes a home-team bounce, you spin and shoot from the hip and luck out. You get back and check yourself over and find a hole in your sleeve but none in your arm, and realize you never felt the tug or heard the whispery crack.

We used to call them John the Wayne days. It does not pay to get overconfident, but you have to ride your luck while you have it. Because it can turn on you.

It had all been a long time ago. The scene had a déjà vu quality. I had been here before in another lifetime, and had killed people I hardly knew.

There was another oncoming sound, a roar, and an airplane came in and flew low and slow, checking the plateau. I eased back down the slope. Even though the paint job was yellow and white instead of the more familiar red and white of Bob Vincent's Cessna at Lauderdale, I knew the model. It was an old utility 206, the Super Skywagon, a durable workhorse with a single Continental 10-520A, fixed tricycle gear with fat tires, able to take six people a thousand miles on eighty-four gallons of fuel, if you babied it along at ten thousand feet at a hundred and thirty miles per hour. I saw two heads through the windshield. I could read off the number on the rudder. N8555F. I could remember Bob bragging about being able to get in and out of a five-hundred-foot strip with a light load.

With no perceptible breeze to worry about, the

pilot went around again and came in. The wheels touched, and he went bounding and braking, kicking up slush, bouncing on the rocky ground. He came to a stop down near the buildings, and I saw Persival and Alvor on the other side of the plane, hurrying toward it. Alvor had his arm around Persival's waist, apparently supporting most of the frail man's weight as he rushed him to the plane. The prop was still turning. I thought they both got in, but could not be sure. There was a pause, probably for shouted explanations, then the plane swiveled around fast and began accelerating down the field for takeoff. Alvor watched it go, then scuttled back to shelter.

I jumped up and ran out. I had both pack straps over my left shoulder, so I could reach into the pack as it dangled under my arm. I reached in for one of those grenades, pulled the pin, and hurled it, trying to lead the airplane, trying to get the grenade out in front of it. I think the pilot saw it and knew what it was. He swerved and lost a little momentum, then picked it up again. The plane bounced one last time and lifted off the rocky stretch.

If I had to guess what happened, I would say that the pilot decided he had lost just enough speed and lift so that he wasn't going to clear the tops of the pines which grew on the downslope beyond the far end of the plateau. The grenade made a harmless crumping sound and a small cloud of dingy smoke far behind the plane. Perhaps it made the pilot nervous, and he started his turn too soon. He wanted to turn left, toward an opening in the trees. Maybe a gust of wind came along just then. The wing tip touched the ground, and that changed the flight attitude of the aircraft. The tail came up a little. He yanked the wing back up, but the plane went down and almost touched wheels again before he tried to lift it over the pines. At the last minute he tried to slip it through but, in slow motion, he sheared the right wing, thick strut, and right wheel off the machine, and it went plunging through the trees, turning, disappearing, then making a prolonged thudding, grinding sound far down the slope. I waited for the sound of gasoline igniting, but it didn't come. If he had the presence of mind, he would have had time to cut the switch.

Alvor had run out of the motor home. I dropped and rolled over and over and over, hugging my weapon in my arms, over the edge of the plateau and down the slope, hearing the fading banshee scream of a ricochet as I came to a stop.

I did some scuttling of my own, moving to my right toward the road. I heard a shouted order, unexpectedly close. I moved beyond a thick tree and stood up. Ahman, Haris, and Alvor were running toward the spot where I had rolled down the slope. They were spread out, about twenty feet separating them, but they were converging. Alvor was making excellent time. They all had weapons at the ready. I guessed they had come up the road just in time to see Alvor fire at me. I clicked my little piece of machinery to full automatic fire. There was enough snow left on the slope so they could track me. I didn't like the idea of lighting out at a dead run for the buildings, hoping to make it. And I had a very brief moment to do some shooting without being shot at. I put as little of me as possible outside the protection of my tree and sprayed them, as with a garden hose, Ahman, the nearest, went down at once, falling hard, losing his weapon. Haris, beyond him, wavered, staggered, and turned, firing in short bursts in my general direction, firing toward the sound before he spotted me. I got behind my tree, snapped a new clip into the weapon, leaned out again, and found Haris shockingly close, lurching like a drunk but firing as he came. A very ballsy performance for a thin man with at least one slug in him. My burst took him squarely in the chest, hammering him back up the few feet of slope and onto the flat, where he fell backward, dead before he could comprehend that finality. A far more authoritative projectile chunked into my tree, and I could imagine that Alvor had one of the assault rifles. I looked around the other side of my tree, a very quick look indeed, but time enough to see Alvor running like a fullback toward the buildings, cutting, feinting, fooling the tacklers. I was moving out to take a chance at him with a long high burst when I saw movement out of the corner of my eye and fired at it immediately, with no pause for conscious thought. Ahman had retrieved his weapon and had been bringing it to bear on me, with every good chance of sending me to join Haris. The burst took him in the higher shoulder, and out of momentary panic I kept the weapon on him, rolling him over and over, a ragged bundle spraying blood and tissue.

A lot of it was luck. A lot of it was having a John Wayne day. But some of it was that old training which eliminates the last hesitation. Death comes while you are struggling with your application or lack of application of the Judeo-Christian ethic. While you work out the equation which says, If I don't kill him, he will kill me, so even if I have been taught not to kill, this is an exception—while you are working that out, he is blowing chunks of bone out of your skull. The quick and the dead is an ancient allusion. They were quick and I was quick and lucky. There was some cunning involved, of course. Being able to see how I might use that tree over the water. Coming back here instead of heading off at a full run. Remembering to scuttle far away from the place where I had rolled out of sight off the plateau. Using Barry as a shield, to shock Chuck momentarily into inaction. So they were gone. Chuck and Barry. The almost-forgotten Nicky. And Persival and the two who had arrived in the plane—probably all dead, from the sound of the impact. Now Haris and Ahman too, leaving only Alvor and the two women. A veritable massacre. A bloodbath. Butchery. I kept the horror bottled away. There would be time to examine that later on. Right now there was the high-riding pleasure of doing some difficult thing far better than you expected to be able to do it. I had been as slow and clumsy as I dared during the exercises. How many of them had died with a feeling of disbelief, frustration, anger? With the ghastly toothy grin of the skull-head of death looking over my shoulder, I was intensely alive. I was alive in every thready little nerve fiber, every capillary. I was tuned to quickness, the world all sharp edges around me, my ears hearing every small sound in the world.

Push the luck. Keep pushing. But the women? I somehow did not think I could open fire from ambush on them, as I had on the others. Had I been as hesitant about the others, I would now be as dead as they were.

I moved along to the head of the road, discarding the nearly empty clip, mounting another. I wanted to be in better position to kill the Dodge van if Alvor should decide to hop in and make a run for the gate. I could guess that he was reasonably certain there was more than one of me. He'd heard the report to Persival about the killing of Chuck and Barry. And he knew the airplane had gone down. Ahman and Haris lay on the thin wet skin of the last of the snow. Rivulets of water ran off the plateau.

I moved across the head of the road and took shelter on the other side. I tried to sort out the people, guess at their assignments. If Ahman and Haris had gone looking for Chuck and Barry, then Sammy was the one I had knocked down with the single slug meant for Alvor. And if they had left somebody on the gate, it would have to be Nena. It was possible Stella was still tied up, that nobody had looked for her in T-6. It was possible that Sammy was waiting for me, armed. Make it four to one, two of them women. But no special advantage to me there—they were as quick and well-trained and toughened as the men had been.

I heard a sudden motion, a slipping sound, then a heavy thud and a grunt, and then a woman said, venomously, "Sonnabitch!" I moved farther back. Sister Nena—I recognized her voice—had been coming up the road and had slipped and fallen. My luck was holding. Water was running down the road through slush and mud. She was watching her footing, but she held the weapon at the ready as she rounded the final bend. I could have shot her then. I held on her and thought of the savage slaughter of the innocent she was quite willing to undertake. I thought of the connection between her and the silvery little sphere which had been used to slay my woman.

I dug a grenade out of the pack. I did not pull the pin. I lobbed it with a slow sidearm so that it would arch over her head and fall on the roadside beyond her. The moment it was in the air, I was on my feet, weapon on the ground. The grenade hit and she spun toward the sound, and I charged her. She heard me coming, but she was caught for a frozen moment in a dilemma of choice. Run from the grenade or turn and cut me down. She ran several steps down the road, tumbled and rolled in expert fashion, and ended up in the prone firing position, getting off one wild shot before I kicked the Uzi out of her hands to turn in the air and land in the shallow wet ditch. I grabbed her, and she came up popping me under the chin with her head so hard the world was full of stars and lights. I turned and took a hard kick on the thigh that could have disabled me. Then she tripped me, somehow, and got loose and went scrambling away, running in a strange fashion on her hands and her feet with her rump high in the air. She had registered that the ring was still affixed to the grenade, and she went after it instead of the Uzi. I tried too fast a start and slipped and went down again. She snatched up the grenade, standing and turning as she did so, yanking the pin, releasing the handle. I saw her lips moving as she counted. Her face was screwed up by the intensity of thought, like a child with a puzzle.

I couldn't get to her. She was moving backward quite rapidly, up the hill. She held her arm back, ready to throw. Whichever way I went, she would lead me, and she was nearing her count. I feinted one way to draw the throw and ran the other way. Just as she tried to throw it underhand, both feet went out from under her and she sat down hard in the slush. She had thrown it and I couldn't see it anywhere. She had a dazed look. I saw it suddenly, coming down. The fall had made her throw it straight up in the air. It hit behind her and bounced off stone, almost as high as her head, before it went off. I weaved my way over to the other ditch, crossed it, and held onto a small tree. It was a good time for Alvor to have happened along, had he only known it. I found my weapon and picked it up, checked it out. I wondered if I was going to be sick. I knew I was not going to look at what was left of Sister Nena. Not now.

How much luck remained to me? I had needed it more with Nena than with any of the others. Her timing had been perfect. A very accurate count. She was planning on an air burst right in my face.

I had the feeling that this had been a warning to me. This is the way They had used up the very last of my luck. All at once. Good-bye, John Wayne. I went around the side of the plateau, around the end, through very difficult country, staying well below the level of the plateau, moving as quietly as I could. Chuck's complicated wristwatch said it was ten o'clock. I had thought it was at least three in the afternoon. I had lived through more bad hours than the watch would admit. Cover and concealment. The day was overcast, and the misty rain began. I had muddied my face. I worked my way up the slope behind the warehouse, walking my forearms along, digging with the toes, watching everything, listening to the dripping eaves, the rain, the silence. It seemed strange to me that I had never heard any birds up here. There should be birds.

Now what would I do if I were old Alvor— Brother Alvor with the broad meaty shoulders, the square gray face? Why, I would set up in a good place. I would set up on a high place. I would, by God, set up on a roof, not necessarily the highest roof around, but one where I could lie doggo, and then pop up suddenly and blow the fisherman to fishbait bits. I looked around very carefully. I backed down the slope and came up in a new place and looked around some more.

Finally I had an idea where I might find him. Persival's motor home had one of those ladders that go up to a depression on top that forms a luggage receptacle, with a little chrome fence around it for the tie-downs. It was a handy place for Alvor. He could have climbed the ladder out of sight of the road area. Yes, it would be a very wise choice. But how to check it out and remain alive? I moved again, back down the slope and up again to where I could come out behind one of the little cement-block structures, out of his sight *if* he were on top of the motor home. I was beginning to get very ragged in the nerve department. I was certain my luck was gone, and so it took just about all I had to stand up and move in close to the wall of the little building. I leaned against it, feeling sweat run out of an armpit and tickle my ribs as it ran down. My hands were shaky. Sammy was waiting in one direction to blow me apart, Stella in another, and Alvor on the high ground. End of the saga. Twilight of the great John Wayne day.

I did not want to leave the shelter of my nice solid little building. It can get to be like when you were a kid, standing on a high place. Wait too long and you can't jump.

Check the weapon. Breathe deeply. Where had all that zest gone? Who stole the gusto? It went when somebody blew the head off Sister Nena.

One way to go at it. I put an eye around the corner of the building. The motor home was right there, about forty feet away. A hide of very thin alloy with an enamel coating. If he was elsewhere, I would be taking the risk of letting him know I was close. But that was acceptable.

I leaned against the building, aimed, let it go on full automatic, cartridge cases dancing away, slugs smacking into the metal, punching holes, making creases in the roundness, making a lot of metallic banging, screech of ricochets, quackety roar of the very rapid cycle of fire. There was an answering roar and something leaped off the roof, out of the depression, and down on the other side of the incongruous vehicle. Have fun on the road. Drive me to Yellowstone. Plug in the water, the electric, and the phone, and adjust the TV aerial.

I had to make my run. But I had a spot right in the middle of my back, right where Sammy or Stella was going to drive it home. I had used the next-to-the-last clip to drive Alvor off the roof, and I put in the last clip when I went hunting him. The silence after all that great rackety clatter was astonishing. I braced my back against the motor home, snapping my head from side to side, wondering if he were already running out across the plateau.

I eased myself down and looked under the vehicle. No feet. I stood up—and felt a faint movement of the whole vehicle, not unlike the slight movement of a heavy boat when somebody steps aboard. Okay, so he had eased the door open and gone in. It moved again. So he was creeping around in there. And might have a shot out of the right window at a steep enough angle to knock off a piece of my head or shoulder. I dropped again and eased under Brother Persival's house. It was a close fit, but I pulled myself slowly, on my back, over to the other side. Now he was in there, peering out the windows, trying to spot me. And I had no idea what in hell I was going to do. All I knew was that I was in a spot where he couldn't see me.

I felt more movement, heard a creak. And then, twenty inches from my head, a muddy shoe came down, stealthily. And the second one as he stepped out of the vehicle. I was dragging the Uzi along by the muzzle, still hot from the long burst, and I knew I had not the time nor the room to pull it to position, aim, and fire it. He stood there, and I reached out and snatched his ankles and pulled them out from under him and tried to snake myself out from under that thing in the same motion. I was halfway out when he kicked me loose. He tried to bring the barrel of his rifle down to bear on me, but I got inside the arc of the muzzle and swarmed onto him, hitting him once in the face. He bucked me off and rolled over and over, but I had hold of the rifle and tore it away from him. I tried to turn it on him, but he came inside the arc just as I had done and butted me up against the side of the vehicle. He was a very powerful man, and a very quick man. I saw the gleam of metal, dropped the rifle, and went for his wrist. We rolled over and over, and I could see that from somewhere he had come up with a stubby, broad-bladed, evil-looking knife. I hate a knife. Then I was on my back and his weight was on me, and with all his strength he was slowly forcing the blade down, bending my arms in the process. I got my feet under me and bucked him off over my head. I snatched his rifle by the barrel and swung the stock at him as he was rolling to his feet. It took him squarely in his thick throat.

His eyes bulged. His face began to change color. He was kneeling, both hands at his throat, tearing the shirt collar away. I could see his chest heaving with the effort to get air through the smashed passageway. His face darkened and his wide eyes saw nothing any more. He sat back on his haunches, then rolled onto his side in the mud, still pulling at his shirt. There was one long rippling, quivering, muscle-jerking spasm, and then he was still. I retrieved the Uzi from under the motor home and stood, listening and listening.

Not luck this time. The strength and the speed of utter, demoralized panic. The extra adrenaline that came from the horror, the terror, of knives.

I went looking, very cautiously, for Sammy. I found him inside the motor home. He sat on the floor, leaning against a pillow. His eyes were half-open. On impulse I closed them with my thumb. The belly and groin and thighs of his coveralls were dark and heavy with blood, the color turning from dark red to chocolate. Evidently one of my slugs had clipped a major artery.

I went to T-6. Somebody had taken the gag out of Stella's mouth and freed her hands and ankles. She was on her back, the edge of the blanket across her waist. She breathed quickly and shallowly. The breathing stopped after every half-dozen or so breaths, and she would be still for perhaps thirty seconds before taking a deep gasping throat-rattling inhalation. I touched the pulse in her throat. It was light and fast. In the dingy light I bent closely and eased her eyelids up. The black pupil of the left one was twice the size of the one of the right eye. I knew the signs. Sister Stella was dying. It is called cerebral hemorrhage.

I looked down at her, and saw her die. Poor sallow little dishwater blonde, a hustler recruited for more serious duty. She had pleasured Brother Thomas. McGee had never touched her. McGee could not remember ever touching her . . . in that direction lies a tantalizingly attractive kind of madness. To become two people means that one need take no responsibility for the other. The pleasant release of guilt or tension can widen the gap between the two.

I covered her to the chin and went out into the blowing mist. There had been ten of them, and two more in the incoming aircraft, and now there were none. I was glad the wind had started again. It was far better than the silence. I shed the belt. I had lost the pack under the motor home. I slung the Uzi over my shoulder. It was comfortable to carry. I went looking for the airplane.

It had gone much farther down the slope than I had supposed. The engine and pieces of the cowling were jammed into a rocky bank. The tail section was up in a tree. The fuselage was in two large parts and dozens of ragged pieces. Seats and bits of plastic and wiring were scattered over a broad area. There was a stink of fuel.

One of them had apparently gone into the rocky bank, as had the engine. He lay bent in wrong directions, missing an arm, and it was impossible to discover what he had looked like. There was a faded tattoo of a blue-and-red eagle on his right wrist, almost obscured by curly blond hair. The eagle held a little scroll in its claws. It said "Charlene."

Another was on his face, and he was draped over a boulder, spread-eagled, hip pockets high. He looked almost normal until I noticed how totally flat his chest was. From back to front he seemed to be about four inches thick. He had huge pale hands. I wanted to see his face, but I didn't care to roll him off his boulder. I sat on my heels, put a hand under his cold chin, and lifted. He had no visible eyelashes or eyebrows. His fine blond hair was cropped short. One small gray eye was open, the other almost closed. A conspiratorial wink. A little mouth, a delicate little nose, and a face pitted and scarred by the acne of his youth.

"And how are you, Brother Titus?" I asked him.

Middling, he seemed to say. Just middling.

"Help!" I dropped Brother Titus's head and scrambled back, tripped, and sat down. "Help me!"

I moved over to the larger part of the wrecked fuselage. Brother Persival lay on his back, on what had been the side wall and windows. The gas stink was stronger.

I made certain his hands were empty before I knelt. He frowned up at me. "McGraw? McGraw, don't touch me. I think my spine is smashed. I can't move my arms and legs."

"Makes quite a problem."

"Get some of the others and rig a litter. If you roll me carefully, you can slide me out of here."

"There aren't any others."

He closed his eyes, then opened them again. "Brother Haris has had some medical training."

"There aren't any others."

"They . . . they ran?" Incredulity.

"They're dead."

After long thoughtful moments he moistened his lips and said, "Then you're a bird dog. You brought a team in."

"No. I'm alone."

"I don't understand. *You* killed them all? How, for God's sake? All those brave young people. Some of our very best. So many thousands of hours and dollars in training them."

"I had a lot of luck. And of course I had some practical experience in their line of work. And motivation. Let's not forget motivation, Brother."

"Who *are* you?"

"I'm Brother Thomas, the commercial fisherman."

"That had become evident. It was checked out. I got word about that yesterday. Who are you?"

"Just your average idle Florida beach bum. Name of McGee. Travis McGee. Salvage consultant." I grinned idiotically at him and stuck my hand out. But of course he couldn't take it. He had closed his eyes. I waited a long time before I touched him on the cheek. "Brother Persival?"

He looked at me. Impatience. "Yes, yes. What is it?"

"Your group killed my woman, in Florida. They went out of their way to give her a death that looked like illness."

"Why would we do that?"

"She had been here a long time ago, looking for her husband's kid sister, and she had seen Titus. Then she saw him again in Fort Lauderdale, negotiating to buy land for some Belgians, and recognized him. They shot a little sphere into the back of her neck and she died."

The look of puzzlement faded. His eyes closed again as he talked. "I don't know about it, of course. But I can see why it could have happened. There are strict rules about security. The friends who are helping us are ruthless about eliminating any link between the religious mission and the political mission. It is perfect cover. I knew we had access to that . . . particular method, but I didn't know it had been used. It was supposed to be undetectable. Odd. Odd. They help the same sort of groups . . . everywhere." He opened his eyes and said, "You came here because of her? Just because of her?"

"Just because of her."

"Strange. To undo so very much. So easily."

The next time I touched him, he didn't respond.

His sleep looked comfortable enough, in the circumstances.

"Just because of her," I told him again. But he was beyond all movement, all reply, all understanding.

15

I worked hard all the rest of that first day of the New Year. I found a bale of coarse blankets in the warehouse. I found some nylon rope and a sharp knife.

The idea, after I went down and made sure the gate was closed and locked, was to recover the farthest bodies first. Chuck and Barry. I took the van down to where I had left the road. It took me longer to find them than I had expected. All the snow was long gone. Spread the blanket. Roll body onto blanket. Tie twice around. Grab corner of blanket near the head and drag back to van. Lift in. Go get the other one. Lift in. Drive up sloppy road to warehouse. Unlock, lift bodies out, drag them inside one at a time. Drag them to place beyond narrow aisle where it widened out again. Side by side near far wall. Neat.

Next, Brother Titus, Brother Persival, and the faceless nameless one-armed third man. Very difficult pulling them up the steep slope. Three in a row. Went and got van. Two into the back, one into the side door. Unlock warehouse, unload, drag them through, one at a time. Five in a row. Neat. But no arm! Went back and looked. Looked everywhere. Finally realized that for some time as I was searching, I had been making a small strange whimpering sound. I put my hand over my mouth and stopped it.

Two out there in the flat. Ahman and Haris. Dragged them one at a time all the way. Easier than lifting, loading, unloading. Seven in a row. But one arm missing. Not as neat as I wanted it to be.

Nena next. Not neat at all. Could not stand the thought of poking about, looking for missing bits. Then Stella. Nine. Easy to drag. Alvor was difficult and bulky to drag. Messy getting Sammy onto the blanket, but okay after that. Eleven of them. Why not twelve? I stood there and counted them, pointing at each one, saying the name. Eleven!

I had missed somebody. Somebody was out there. I counted them over and over, and I was beginning to make that noise again. And then I remembered the twelfth. Nicky. Executed by me. Buried by his comrades.

Not much of the fading daylight came in. I sat on a crate purporting to contain electronic equipment. Eleven silent ones. I felt a strange affection for them. They were so docile. This was my own tiny little Jonestown. We had shared together the final climactic emotional experience. Did dark shadows move within the fading electrical charges of the emptied minds? Did the final instant record on continuous replay, over and over, each playing dimmer?

I got up and felt my way out and locked them in, safe for the night. They'd had a very bad day, but they were safe for the night. Luck had run against them. John Wayne had deserted them.

I found two big flashlights, camp lanterns. I did not want to fool with the generator. I didn't want to listen to it. I went down to the creek with soap and towels, aimed the lanterns, and bathed and scrubbed in the black slide of ice water. I dressed in fresh coveralls, went to a trailer where nobody lived and where nobody had died, and rolled up in three blankets—rolled onto my clenched fist to ease the hollowness of my empty belly—and slept twelve hours without dreaming, without waking, without, as far as I could tell, moving at all.

In the morning I was able to eat. Then I went collecting. I looked for books, notebooks, tape decks, tapes, letters, documents, money, identification. Brother Persival had the team's petty cash in a lockbox in the bottom of his hanging locker. Almost thirty-six thousand. It all fitted reasonably well into the double lining of my old duffel bag. I remembered the airplane and went back to the wreck and hunted until I found the flight log. It was damp with evaporating gasoline but legible. Dates, engine hours, destinations—some in the clear, some in code. Passengers and freight carried. Clear and coded. Fuel consumption. Estimated payloads. Maybe somebody could decipher where it had been and thus find some of the rest of these little warrens of Brothers and Sisters waiting to be blooded. I found the flight log, but not the arm. I walked farther afield, looking for it. I studied the trees, looking up at the crotches and crevices. No arm. Not one. Anywhere.

There were very few documents. It was as if they had been ordered to keep nothing personal. Everything I found fitted into one large suitcase from Alvor's cement house. It was black metal, like those carried by immigrants in old movies.

I had washed out the van. It had not been in bad shape. The blankets had saved it. I put my duffel bag in the van. I put the suitcase in the van. In one of the travel trailers I had found a big shiny old-fashioned alarm clock. I took it into the warehouse. I did not go all the way through to where the bodies were. I tested the alarm. It was very loud. I had located one case of six rockets. I set the alarm for five hours in the future, which would make it six in the evening. I uncapped six rockets, aimed them into different parts of the storage piles, jammed them in firmly. I took off the little acoustic caps. Just turn the switches and tiptoe out. I looked and thought, then screwed the acoustic caps back on and put the rockets back in the case, walked out and threw the alarm clock as far as I could, relocked the warehouse, and left.

I drove down to the gate, unlocked it, drove out, locked it behind me. The morning had been muggy. The afternoon was colder. I drove a black van with big gold crosses on the side. I tried to look pious and preoccupied. The second day of a brand-new year. I tried to hurry, but every time I looked at the speedometer, I was back down to thirty miles an hour. It seemed fast enough.

I found a big gas station near Ukiah. I got change from the office and placed the call to the memorized number.

It rang three times and a hushed voice, male, said, "Hello."

"Was someone . . . was someone at this number trying to reach Travis McGee?"

"I can try to find out for you."

"If you find out they were, I can be reached at this number." I read it off the pay phone.

"If they were trying to reach you, they'll call back."

I had parked the van next to the phone booth. I

sat where I could hear the ring. At four o'clock the man came out from the station. "Are you okay?"

"I'm waiting for a call."

"All this time?"

"I'm waiting for a call."

He looked me over carefully. "You sure you're all right?"

"I'm fine. I'm fine."

After that he would come out of the building about every fifteen minutes and stare over at me.

At 6:10 P.M. the phone rang. I moved quickly and shut myself in the booth.

"Hello?"

"McGee?"

"Yes. Are you Max or Jake?"

"Neither. But I know what went on."

"Can you prove that?"

"If you can think of a way, maybe I can."

"I was with a friend. He stayed outside. We used a code."

"Hold on. I saw that in here somewhere. Here it is. The word hat. To mean a weapon. Bring your hat."

"Okay. I think somebody better get here. I think they better get here fast. I keep kind of slipping off, in a funny way."

"Where are you?"

"Near Ukiah, near an off ramp, near a Shell station. Ukiah, California."

"Because you call, we should come?"

"I hope you're recording this, pal. Because I don't feel like going over it if you don't believe it. Brother Titus is dead. And Brother Persival and ten more of them. They're in a warehouse up in the hills. The warehouse is full of weapons, ammo, incendiaries, plastique, grenades, rockets. They were terrorists who trained all over the world and they—"

"Hold it! Can you see a motel anywhere near you?"

I looked around. "Talmadge Lodge."

"You have cash?"

"Enough."

"Go there and check in. And wait."

"I'll use the name of Thomas McGraw. How long will I have to wait?"

"I'd guess until six tomorrow morning. Or seven. I want to get the two you met back in on this thing. They're . . . pretty far away."

There were nine of them, in three nondescript cars, and they did not want to waste any time sitting around chatting. They seemed to be under intense strain. I was in the lead car with Jake at the wheel, pointing out the way. Max leaned over from the back seat. "Why the hell did you come out here?"

"Why not?"

"People like you can screw everything up."

"So why didn't you get out here first?"

"It was way down the list. We'd have gotten around to it. We're understaffed. Jesus Christ, McGee, each one of us is doing the work of three men. The government solution to a problem is throw money at it. So what do you do when you can't really mention the problem?"

"Why the big rush? Everything is still there."

Jake said, "We've gotten to too many places right after the moving men have cleaned it out."

I thought I had missed one turn, but I hadn't. I unlocked the gate, swung it open, and got back in. The three cars went barreling up the narrow steep road, sliding on the greasy turns. All the structures were there. The silence was there. I pointed out the building.

I unlocked the door for them and stepped back out of the way and let them go in. I went back and leaned on a car. In five minutes two of them came out, looking a little green. Max was one of them. After they breathed in some fresh air they went back in. Ten minutes later Max came out, another man following him with a notebook.

"—and I want unmarked trucks up here, with secure drivers. The biggest that can make that last hill and the curves. They'll take the long way around from here to Fort Bragg and go into classified storage. Our people will look at the stuff there to see if there's anything new and different. Got that?"

"Got it."

"I want to sneak a helicopter in here big enough to fly out with eleven bodies. They should bring body bags and some graves registration people. Secure people, of course."

"Got it."

"I want them taken to Home Town fastest. I want a priority on those pix and prints they're taking in there. They should be about ready to give them to you, and then you can take off. Who's got that black tin suitcase?"

"It's in the trunk of Red's car."

"They'll fly back with us to Home Town, and when you're setting the other stuff up, make sure they get good people on E. and A. Take them off other stuff if necessary. Now read back, just the highlights."

"Mmm. Unmarked trucks, secure drivers, classified storage at Bragg. Bodies out on helicopter. Body bags and graves registration people, direct to Home Town. Priority on the pix and prints, and I take them in. Take black suitcase out with me . . . no, that goes with you. What I do is get Evaluation and Analysis primed to go when it gets there."

That was all. He went back into the warehouse. Max motioned to me, and we strolled across the flats. I told him I would show him where the airplane went in.

"So many of them," he said. "Jesus!"

"I know."

"Are you all right?"

"I don't know what the hell it is. Like some kind of combat fatigue. Look at my hand shake. It was a long time ago, and it all came back at once."

"You went kind of crazy?"

"No. Not like that. I was—pretty calm, actually. I mean you go along and you figure the odds of doing this and the odds against doing that, and whatever you do, you make it sudden and final."

"You say three were in the Cessna? So you waxed eight of them."

"Nine. There's one buried over a week ago. Nicky. They gave me the gun and told me to shoot him and I did. That was what started all the rest of it. Like letting some kind of bad spell out of the bottle. I thought it was a fake execution, so I fired and killed him."

We got to the slope and looked down to where we could see bits of the airplane. "I got all the records out of there I could find," I said. "And I looked everywhere for that goddamn missing arm. I looked high and low. I can't imagine how it hid itself so damn well." My voice was getting high and thin, but I couldn't seem to stop. "Somehow we've got to find that damn arm!"

"Hey," he said. "Hey, fellow. Take it easy, huh?" He turned me around and headed me back toward the cars. "I'll have some of my guys go down there and find it."

We walked in silence.

"How'd you get them all?"

I used as few words as possible.

He gave me a strange sidelong look. I've seen people at the zoo look at the big cats that way, as if they are wondering if the creature could bang right through those bars if he felt like it.

"You're going to have to come back for debriefing."

"Debrief somebody who was never briefed?"

"It's just a word we use, McGee. I think they'll go at you for a week or more. It won't be bad. You'll get good food and rest. The motivation people will want to know just about every word those people spoke to you."

"The one they should talk to is Sister Elena Marie. She used to be Bobbie Jo Annison, the evangelist."

"We know. We'd like to talk to her for a long long time. And the people who pull her strings, and write her words. We think she's on an island off the south coast of Cuba. Maybe there'll be a lead in those papers. You shouldn't have gathered them up for us."

"I did that when I was going to blow the whole place to rubble, buildings, people, and all. I was saving the papers for you and Jake. I collected all the money. I think I was saving that for myself. Some of it is mine, about nine thousand. Some twenty-seven thousand is theirs."

"I can't understand why they didn't kill you out

of hand. That's their style. That's their standard program. No infiltration. No way to do it."

"I was looking for my daughter."

"Daughter!"

"I'm sorry. I'm past making much sense."

"We'll leave here soon. It's a strain on you, having to stay here."

"Can we stop in San Francisco? I left my ID there, and my clothes."

"Of course. You're not under detention."

"For murder?"

"For self-defense. We'll let the record read there was a jurisdictional squabble and they fought among themselves. Look, you should be getting a medal, McGee. But what you are going to get is some very serious and earnest advice about keeping your mouth shut forever. I think you cut down their firepower and manpower some. If the documents give us a lead to other camps, we can cut it down some more. But the summer timetable is probably still on. They can't keep their tigers waiting forever. And they have to have something to show the folks helping them from overseas. No matter how much security we lay on, they are going to create one hell of a series of bloody messes from border to border and coast to coast. A lot of sweet dumb people are going to get ripped up. Headlines, speeches, doom, the end of our way of life, and so on. Terrorism is going to pay us one big fat bloody visit, McGee. But it will only be a visit. They underestimate our national resilience. Aroused by that kind of savagery, we can become a very tough kind of people. You are a pretty good example of that."

"My luck was running, and I let it run."

"They were supposed to be their best, huh? Educated abroad. Honed fine. During the debriefing, you'll have to go into infinite detail about the training, what you saw of it."

"Everything I can remember."

"They'll want to go into hypnotic drugs to make sure they pull everything out."

"I'm in no position to object."

He stopped walking and turned to face me. "And when it is over and they turn you loose, all the information stops, then and there. You never get any more from us, and nobody ever gets any of what you have from you."

"Except Meyer."

"Nobody!"

"Except Meyer."

"I am serious, dammit!"

"Me too. So you better not turn me loose. There is no way on earth that I can keep from telling him every damn detail of every damn day I spent here. Can't you remember the clearance he used to have? You checked it out. Remember?"

"Oh, hell, yes. Okay. Meyer. And only Meyer."

Two of them came out and spoke to Max in low

voices. He came over to me and said, "Take your last look around. And hope they never find out who did their people in."

"I think they know."

"If I was sure they know, I would set up a whole new identity for you, from plastic surgery to colored contact lenses."

"I wouldn't accept it anyway."

"You don't care if they come after you?"

"Frankly, not a hell of a lot, Max. Not a hell of a lot."

In a little while we headed down out of the hills. Jake told me that when everything had been taken out, they were going to truck a couple of bulldozers up there and knock everything flat and push it off the edge. I said that would be nice. They said we would stay overnight in San Francisco, so I could rest up a little, and fly out in the morning. I said that would be nice. They said that maybe the money problem could be resolved in my favor. Like a kind of unofficial reward. Like, maybe, a bounty. I said that would be nice. So they stopped talking to me. I looked out the car window at the tall evergreens and wondered why all the birds had left this part of the world. Jake turned the wipers on, smearing the small sad rain. I think they were glad to stop trying to relate to me. They felt uneasy about me, about being close to me in a small car. I think they felt not exactly certain of what I might do next. And I knew they would not have felt better about it if I had told them I didn't have the faintest notion, either, of what I might do next, today, tomorrow, or ever.

Epilogue

We had found a little cove around behind the Berry Islands, and with the small chop slapping us in the transom, I had bumped twice getting over the bar into the still water. But that was at low tide, and the charts for that day in late June said it was unusually low, so no sweat about getting out, getting that absolute jewel of a cruiser out of there.

It was named *Odalisque III*, and it was the splendid playtoy of Lady Vivian Stanley-Tucker of St. Kitts. It was a fifty-three-foot Magnum Maltese Flybridge cruiser, built in North Miami Beach. Twin turbocharged diesels cruised it at an honest thirty miles an hour. Paneling, radar, recording fathometer, air conditioning, ice-maker, tub and shower, huge master stateroom, double autopilot system, stereo music, wine locker, microwave oven, live wells, loran, pile carpeting. I knew it would knock close to a half million without extras, and it was the third time her husband had given her a boat for her birthday.

"The other two were huuuuuge!" she had said. "Great vulgar monsters. Had to have a crew aboard at all times. Now this one is cozy, what? Intimate, you might say. The old boy was playing the gold market and got pinched a bit. Apologized for the smaller boat."

I was over on the beach and had found a sandbar that was supporting more than its share of clams. Lady Vivian and I had been out about two weeks, provisions were running a little short, and soon we would have to decide whether to put in to Nassau or run on over to Miami. I was putting the clams in a string bag. The sun felt needle-hot on my bare back. I was turning saddle brown, and Lady Vivian had turned to a very lovely reddish gold, except for the sunburned tip of her nose.

The deep chord of the air horns made me look out toward the *Odalisque*. Shave and a haircut, two bits. Then she came out onto the bow, a tiny golden figure in a white bikini, and motioned me to come aboard.

I hung the string bag around my neck, swam out through the warm crystal-clear water, and came up the boarding ladder.

"Good nap?"

"Splendid! And I felt absolutely marvelous until, like the dutiful person I am, I turned on the thing-ajiggy at call time, as usual, and damn me if the old bustard wasn't trying to get me. Baaaaad news, sweet McGeeee. I have to fly on down. His damned awful sister has decided to come out for a visit, and he thinks it would look most odd if I'm not there to greet the old party. So what I told him, I would go on into Nassau tomorrow and fly from there, and find some dear friend who'll take the *Odalisque* on over to Lauderdale. Who might that dear friend be?"

"Give me a hint."

"Damn, I was having such a lovely time. And we're getting so horribly healthy. All this popping into bed must be awfully good for one."

Though tiny in the distance, she was substantial up close, a green-eyed, toffee-haired woman just barely on the sunny side of forty, if you could believe her. She gave the healthy impression of someone about to burst out of her clothes, and in fact was willing so to do when the provocation was sufficiently explicit. She had very fine-textured skin, gentle as cream, and her body temperature seemed to run permanently at about four degrees above normal. In bed she was like a stove. She radiated both heat and need.

I put the clams away for later, washed up, and then mixed us a pair of the sour rum drinks she doted on. We sat out on the afterdeck under the tarp I had rigged for shade.

We touched glasses, and as she sipped, she smiled with her eyes.

"So, there will be another cruise at least," she said.

"As long as I can last."

"You are a dear man. I see no sign of faltering, as yet."

"I sneak megadoses of vitamins, Viv."

"You are the only person in this whole wide world I have ever allowed to call me Viv. Why do I like it when you say it?"

"Because you are helplessly in love with me."

That got a hoot of laughter, her great bawdy laugh of derision. "You know, dearest McGeeee, I would feel a great deal better if I'd been able to pin you down about really helping us."

"I don't think I could do any good."

"Utter nonsense! You could do it easily, probably. It was my money, you know, not Sir Charles's. From my Uncle Merriman. His people made it in the War of the Roses, or some bloody thing like that, selling slop to both sides, I imagine. After death duties, not very much came down to me, as you can imagine. But it was *comforting*. You would know. You wake in the night and think of something that you might want, and you know you can *buy* it. It was truly a magnificent necklace. For forty thousand pounds, it had to be. And somehow,

The Green Ripper

between appraisals, that wretched little animal switched it on us and now pretends to know nothing about it, and there is nothing we can do. Should you get it back for us, dear heart, we shall auction it at Christie's and give you half the gavel price. Your customary arrangement, isn't it?"

"When I work, it is. I work when I need money. Otherwise I am retired. Like now."

"Ha! Living off my involuntary generosity? Last night the only possible roll to escape a double gammon was that incredible six four you rolled. Dear, I am really terribly serious about the necklace. Would you try? For me? For jolly old Viv?"

"Why not? I'll need the one he substituted, probably. I'll try to work something out."

"Bless you!"

And the great warm tide of her pleasure and her gratitude took us down into the cool humming, buzzing grotto of the *Odalisque* below decks, into the deep bunk—leaving behind us on the carpeting a hasty trail of bikini top, swim trunks, and bikini bottom—where, with the accompaniment of her giggles and sighs and little instructional signals, we played our favorite game of winding up that luxurious engine of a body of hers to such an aching pitch that a single slight touch, carefully planned, pushed her over the edge. After that, as always, she went into lazy yawning, smiles, a gentle kiss, and her deep deep sleep.

I picked up the discarded clothing, put on my

trunks, and quietly fixed an oversized old-fashioned glass full of ice and Boodles. Sipping size. I went topside to the fly bridge, lounged on the padded bench in the fading heat of the late afternoon sun.

I remembered how it had been when I had come back home to Bahia Mar, to *The Busted Flush*, in mid-February, after the teams of skilled interrogators had pulled every last scrap of information, no matter how trivial or unrelated, out of the stubborn tangle in the back of my mind. It took me a week to tell Meyer all of it, at my own pace, quitting whenever I came up against something that needed more thought before I could talk about it willingly.

Meyer had been patient and understanding and, best of all, willing to believe what I still considered unbelievable.

"Travis, did you get any clue at all about whether they can stop the other teams?"

"I saw Max and Jake one more time, a few days before they let me come home. They let me ask some questions. They didn't answer a lot of them. They'd acted quickly enough to terminate a few of the training centers, but the rest of them moved out in time. At best it will push the target date further into the future. Maybe it will begin to happen a year from now."

"What about that Brussels thing?"

"A dead end. It was probably going to be one of their restaging areas, for retraining and re-equipping the survivors of the early strikes."

"And Gretel had the bad luck to see Titus. That was why they . . . did away with her?"

"He was the link between the Church of the Apocrypha and the terrorist arm. They had a fat file on him, but not as an important wheel in the Church. Now the Church has gone underground. That cripples the financing. They probably over-reacted. If they had just given up the land purchase, forfeited the payment, it would have been enough. What could Gretel have done, other than tell Ladwigg she had recognized his visitor? Overkill. Paranoia. Maybe just an urge to test a new deadly toy."

"Who did kill her?"

"Nobody seems to know. Or care very much. It wasn't anything particularly personal, killing her or Ladwigg. It was just a case of trying to tidy up a security lapse."

"Will you be told anything more?"

" 'There's no need ever to contact me again,' Jake said."

"Are you sure you're all right?" Meyer asked earnestly.

"I don't know how I am. Or exactly who I am."

"Remember when I talked about the new barbarism last December? About the toad-lizard thing with the rotten breath, squatting in its cave? You met it, Travis. You felt the lizard breath. It is man's primal urge to decimate himself down to numbers which can exist on the wornout planet. It is man's self-hatred. The god of the lemmings, and of the poisonous creatures which can die of their own venom. It takes time to back away from that, Travis. Time."

It had taken most of the five months to finish the job of sorting myself out. Meyer had put me on the right track. I didn't know what he had meant when he said to me, "Not one of us ever grows up to be what he intended to be. Not one of us fulfills his own expectations, Travis. We are all our own children, in that sense. At some point, somewhere, we have to stop making demands."

There was no great moment of my saying, "Aha!" or "Eureka!" It just slowly came clear, like the mist rising on a mountain morning. There was a black, deep, dreadful ravine separating me from all my previous days. Over there on the other side were the pathetic and innocent little figures of world-that-once-was. McGee and his chums. McGee and Gretel. McGee and his toys and visions.

I could not approach the edge of that ravine and look down. Far far below were the bodies of the dead.

And here I was, on this side. This side was today. This side was the crystal taste of icy gin, the brute weight of tropic sun, the tiny beads of sweat on my forearm, the lovely lines of the Magnum Maltese, those white popcorn gulls way out there, afloat after feeding, Viv's glad little cries of love, the way the stars would shine tonight, the way the clams would taste, the way we would fit together as we slept.

I tasted all the tastes of today and felt in me a rising joy that this could be true. I had raised myself up from many madnesses to be exactly what I am. It had become too constant a pain to try endlessly to be what I thought I should become.

I thought I saw movement over toward the shallows, sixty feet away, where the water danced in sunlight. I looked in the drawer and took out the Polaroid glasses and put them on. Yes, there were some bonefish tailing across the grass, feeding. I went down and changed the rig on the little Orvis spinner, knifed open a clam for bait, sneaked out near the transom and was barely able to drop the clam far enough ahead of them so as not to spook them.

For a little while I thought they would feed right on by, but then came the soft mouthy movement. I counted to three and gave him a quick little hit, and he took off, screaming the reel, hissing the line. There is an almost indescribable elegance about that first run of a big bonefish. Big meaning anything from five pounds to ten. No flap, no wobble, just incredibly smooth acceleration. He circled from the port quarter around the stern about a hundred feet from the boat, and around to starboard. I had no hope of turning him. I managed to pass the rod around the aerial and outrigger without losing him, but I could not manage to get up the ladderway to the bridge fast enough to clear the line, and he broke loose. I laughed at myself, and I wished the fish good luck and long life. His acids would dissolve the hook within days. He would have something to tell the others. How he outwitted monsters.

I stowed the rod and went back up to the gin. The sun was moving down toward the horizon, losing some of its sting. Viv came climbing up to the fly bridge, glass in hand. She was wearing a short beach robe with big red polkadots. She kissed me. She smelled of her French soap, and tasted of her mint toothpaste. She put her drink down, combed her hands back through her hair and stretched on tiptoe, then sat down, sipped her drink, and smiled at me.

No need for words. Her eyes were wishing me luck and long life. I had outwitted monsters.

About the author:

John D. MacDonald, says *The New York Times*, "is a very good writer, not just a good 'mystery writer.'" His Travis McGee novels (of which this is the eighteenth) have established their hero as a modern-day Sam Spade and, along with MacDonald's more than 500 short stories and other best-selling novels—60 in all, including *Condominium* —have stamped their author as one of America's best all-round contemporary storytellers.

JOHN D. MACDONALD

"The king of the adventure novel" John D. MacDonald is one of the world's most popular authors of mystery and suspense. Here he is at his bestselling best.

CONDOMINIUM	23525	$2.25
ALL THESE CONDEMNED	14239	$1.50
APRIL EVIL	14128	$1.75
BALLROOM OF THE SKIES	14143	$1.75
THE BEACH GIRLS	14081	$1.75
THE BRASS CUPCAKE	14141	$1.75
A BULLET FOR CINDERELLA	14106	$1.75
CANCEL ALL OUR VOWS	13764	$1.75
CLEMMIE	14015	$1.75
CONTRARY PLEASURE	14104	$1.75
THE CROSSROADS	14033	$1.75
DEADLOW TIDE	14166	$1.75
DEADLY WELCOME	13682	$1.50
DEATH TRAP	13557	$1.50
THE DECEIVERS	14016	$1.75
THE DROWNERS	13582	$1.75
THE EMPTY TRAP	14185	$1.75
THE END OF THE NIGHT	14192	$1.75
THE LAST ONE LEFT	13958	$1.95

This offer expires 2/28/81   8004-2